THE GHOST PIRATES

THE GHOST PIRATES

William Hope Hodgson

Contents

THE FIGURE OUT OF THE SEA

He began without any circumlocution.

I joined the Mortzestus in 'Frisco. I heard before I signed on, that there were some funny yarns floating round about her; but I was pretty nearly on the beach, and too jolly anxious to get away, to worry about trifles. Besides, by all accounts, she was right enough so far as grub and treatment went. When I asked fellows to give it a name, they generally could not. All they could tell me, was that she was unlucky, and made thundering long passages, and had no more than a fair share of dirty weather. Also, that she had twice had the sticks blown out of her, and her cargo shifted. Besides all these, a heap of other things that might happen to any packet, and would not be comfortable to run into. Still, they were the ordinary things, and I was willing enough to risk them, to get home. All the same, if I had been given the chance, I should have shipped in some other vessel as a matter of preference.

When I took my bag down, I found that they had signed on the rest of the crowd. You see, the "home lot" cleared out when they got into 'Frisco, that is, all except one young fellow, a cockney, who had stuck by the ship in port. He told me afterwards, when I got to know him, that he intended to draw a pay-day out of her, whether any one else did, or not.

The first night I was in her, I found that it was common talk among the other fellows, that there was something queer about the ship. They spoke of her as if it were an accepted fact that she was haunted; yet they all treated the matter as a joke; all, that is, except the young cockney—Williams—who, instead of laughing at their jests on the subject, seemed to take the whole matter seriously.

This made me rather curious. I began to wonder whether there was, after all, some truth underlying the vague stories I had heard; and I took the first opportunity to ask him whether he had any reasons for believing that there was anything in the yarns about the ship.

At first he was inclined to be a bit offish; but, presently, he came round, and told me that he did not know of any particular incident which could be called unusual in the sense in which I meant. Yet that, at the same time, there were lots of little things which, if you put them together, made you think a bit. For instance, she always made such long passages and had so much dirty weather—nothing but that and calms and head winds. Then, other things happened; sails that he knew, himself, had been properly stowed, were always blowing adrift at night. And then he said a thing that surprised me.

"There's too many bloomin' shadders about this 'ere packet; they gets onter yer nerves like nothin' as ever I seen before in me nat'ral."

He blurted it all out in a heap, and I turned round and looked at him.

"Too many shadows!" I said. "What on earth do you mean?" But he refused to explain himself or tell me anything further—just shook his head, stupidly, when I questioned him. He seemed to have taken a sudden, sulky fit. I felt certain that he was acting dense, purposely. I believe the truth of the matter is that he was, in a way, ashamed of having let himself go like he had, in speaking out his thoughts about "shadders." That type of man may think things at times; but he doesn't often put them into words. Anyhow, I saw it was no use asking any further questions; so I let the matter drop there. Yet, for several days afterwards, I caught myself wondering, at times, what the fellow had meant by "shadders."

We left 'Frisco next day, with a fine, fair wind, that seemed a bit like putting the stopper on the yarns I had heard about the ship's ill luck. And yet—

He hesitated a moment, and then went on again.

For the first couple of weeks out, nothing unusual happened, and the wind still held fair. I began to feel that I had been rather lucky, after all, in the packet into which I had been shunted. Most of the other fellows gave her a good name, and there was a pretty general opinion growing among the crowd, that it was all a silly yarn about her being haunted. And then, just when I was settling down to things, something happened that opened my eyes no end.

It was in the eight to twelve watch, and I was sitting on the steps, on the starboard side, leading up to the fo'cas'le head. The night was fine and there was a splendid moon. Away aft, I heard the timekeeper strike four bells, and the look-out, an old fellow named Jaskett, answered him. As he let go the bell lanyard, he caught sight of me, where I sat quietly, smoking. He leant over the rail, and looked down at me.

"That you, Jessop?" he asked.

"I believe it is," I replied.

"We'd 'ave our gran'mothers an' all the rest of our petticoated relash'ns comin' to sea, if 'twere always like this," he remarked, reflectively—indicating, with a sweep of his pipe and hand, the calmness of the sea and sky.

I saw no reason for denying that, and he continued:

"If this ole packet is 'aunted, as some on 'em seems to think, well all as I can say is, let me 'ave the luck to tumble across another of the same sort. Good grub, an' duff fer Sundays, an' a decent crowd of 'em aft, an' everythin' comfortable like, so as yer can feel yer knows where yer are. As fer 'er bein' 'aunted, that's all 'ellish nonsense. I've comed 'cross lots of 'em before as was said to be 'aunted, an' so some on 'em was; but 'twasn't with ghostesses. One packet I was in, they was that bad yer couldn't sleep a wink in yer watch below, until yer'd 'ad every stitch out yer bunk an' 'ad a reg'lar 'unt. Sometimes—" At that moment, the relief, one of the ordinary seamen, went up the other ladder on to the fo'cas'le head, and the old chap turned to ask him "Why the 'ell" he'd not relieved him a bit smarter. The ordinary made some reply; but what it was, I did not catch; for, abruptly, away aft, my rather sleepy gaze had lighted on something altogether extraordinary and outrageous. It was nothing less than the form of a man stepping inboard over the starboard rail, a little abaft the main rigging. I stood up, and caught at the handrail, and stared.

Behind me, someone spoke. It was the look-out, who had come down off the fo'cas'le head, on his way aft to report the name of his relief to the second mate.

"What is it, mate?" he asked, curiously, seeing my intent attitude.

The thing, whatever it was, had disappeared into the shadows on the lee side of the deck.

"Nothing!" I replied, shortly; for I was too bewildered then, at what my eyes had just shown me, to say any more. I wanted to think.

The old shellback glanced at me; but only muttered something, and went on his way aft.

For a minute, perhaps, I stood there, watching; but could see nothing. Then I walked slowly aft, as far as the after end of the deck house. From there, I could see most of the main deck; but nothing showed, except, of course, the moving shadows of the ropes and spars and sails, as they swung to and fro in the moonlight.

The old chap who had just come off the look-out, had returned forrard again, and I was alone on that part of the deck. And then, all at once, as I stood peering into the shadows to leeward, I remembered what Williams had said about there being too many "shadders." I had been puzzled to understand his real meaning, then. I had no difficulty now. There were too many shadows. Yet, shadows or no shadows, I realised that for my own peace of mind, I must settle, once and for all, whether the thing I had seemed to see stepping aboard out of the ocean, had been a reality, or simply a phantom, as you might say, of my imagination. My reason said it was nothing more than imagination, a rapid dream—I must have dozed; but something deeper than reason told me that this was not so. I put it to the test, and went straight in amongst the shadows— There was nothing.

I grew bolder. My common sense told me I must have fancied it all. I walked over to the mainmast, and looked behind the pinrail that partly surrounded it, and down into the shadow of the pumps; but here again was nothing. Then I went in under the break of the poop. It was darker under there than out on deck. I looked up both sides of the deck, and saw that they were bare of anything such as I looked for. The assurance was comforting. I glanced at the poop ladders, and remembered that nothing could have gone up there, without the Second Mate or the Time-keeper seeing it. Then I leant my back up against the bulkshead, and thought the whole matter over, rapidly, sucking at my pipe, and keeping my glance about the deck. I concluded my think, and said "No!" out loud. Then something occurred to me, and I said "Unless—" and went over to the starboard bulwarks, and looked over and down into the sea; but there was nothing but sea; and so I turned and made my way forrard. My common sense had triumphed, and I was convinced that my imagination had been playing tricks with me.

I reached the door on the portside, leading into the fo'cas'le, and was about to enter, when something made me look behind. As I did so, I had a shaker. Away aft, a dim, shadowy form stood in the wake of a swaying belt of moonlight, that swept the deck a bit abaft the main-mast.

It was the same figure that I had just been attributing to my fancy. I will admit that I felt more than startled; I was quite a bit frightened. I was convinced now that it was no mere imaginary thing. It was a human figure. And yet, with the flicker of the moonlight and the shadows chasing over it, I was unable to say more than that. Then, as I stood there, irresolute and funky, I got the thought that someone was acting the goat; though for what reason or purpose, I never stopped to consider. I was glad of any suggestion that my common sense assured me was not impossible; and, for the moment, I felt quite relieved. That side to the question had not presented itself to me before. I began to pluck up courage. I accused myself of getting fanciful; otherwise I should have tumbled to it earlier. And then, funnily enough, in spite of all my reasoning, I was still afraid of going aft to discover who that was, standing on the lee side of the maindeck. Yet I felt that if I shirked it, I was only fit to be dumped overboard; and so I went, though not with any great speed, as you can imagine.

I had gone half the distance, and still the figure remained there, motionless and silent—the moonlight and the shadows playing over it with each roll of the ship. I think I tried to be surprised. If it were one of the fellows playing the fool, he must have heard me coming, and why didn't he scoot while he had the chance? And where could he have hidden himself, before? All these things, I asked myself, in a rush, with a queer mixture of doubt and belief; and, you know, in the meantime, I was drawing nearer. I had passed the house, and was not twelve paces distant; when, abruptly, the silent figure made three quick strides to the port rail, and climbed over it into the sea.

I rushed to the side, and stared over; but nothing met my gaze, except the shadow of the ship, sweeping over the moonlit sea.

How long I stared down blankly into the water, it would be impossible to say; certainly for a good minute. I felt blank—just horribly blank. It was such a beastly confirmation of the unnaturalness of the thing I had concluded to be only a sort of brain fancy. I seemed, for that little time, deprived, you know, of the power of coherent thought. I suppose I was dazed—mentally stunned, in a way.

As I have said, a minute or so must have gone, while I had been staring into the dark of the water under the ship's side. Then, I came suddenly to my ordinary self. The Second Mate was singing out: "Lee fore brace."

I went to the braces, like a chap in a dream.

What Tammy the Prentice Saw

The next morning, in my watch below, I had a look at the places where that strange thing had come aboard, and left the ship; but I found nothing unusual, and no clue to help me to understand the mystery of the strange man.

For several days after that, all went quietly; though I prowled about the decks at night, trying to discover anything fresh that might tend to throw some light on the matter. I was careful to say nothing to any one about the thing I had seen. In any case, I felt sure I should only have been laughed at.

Several nights passed away in this manner, and I was no nearer to an understanding of the affair. And then, in the middle watch, something happened.

It was my wheel. Tammy, one of the first voyage 'prentices, was keeping time—walking up and down the lee side of the poop. The Second Mate was forrard, leaning over the break of the poop, smoking. The weather still continued fine, and the moon, though declining, was sufficiently powerful to make every detail about the poop, stand out distinctly. Three bells had gone, and I'll admit I was feeling sleepy. Indeed, I believe I must have dozed, for the old packet steered very easily, and there was precious little to do, beyond giving her an odd spoke now and again. And then, all at once, it seemed to me that I heard someone calling my name, softly. I could not be certain; and first I glanced forrard to where the Second stood, smoking, and from him, I looked into the binnacle. The ship's head was right on her course, and I felt easier. Then, suddenly, I heard it again. There was no doubt about it this time, and I glanced to leeward. There I saw Tammy reaching over the steering gear, his hand out, in the act of trying to touch my arm. I was about to ask him what the devil he wanted, when he held up his finger for silence, and pointed forrard along the lee side of the poop. In the dim light, his face showed palely, and he seemed much agitated. For a few seconds, I stared in the direction he indicated, but could see nothing.

"What is it?" I asked in an undertone, after a couple of moments' further ineffectual peering. "I can't see anything."

"H'sh!" he muttered, hoarsely, without looking in my direction. Then, all at once, with a quick little gasp, he sprang across the wheel-box, and stood beside me, trembling. His gaze appeared to follow the movements of something I could not see.

I must say that I was startled. His movement had shown such terror; and the way he stared to leeward made me think he saw something uncanny.

"What the deuce is up with you?" I asked, sharply. And then I remembered the Second Mate. I glanced forrard to where he lounged. His back was still towards us, and he had not seen Tammy. Then I turned to the boy.

"For goodness sake, get to looard before the Second sees you!" I said. "If you want to say anything, say it across the wheel-box. You've been dreaming."

Even as I spoke, the little beggar caught at my sleeve with one hand; and, pointing across to the log-reel with the other, screamed: "He's coming! He's coming—" At this instant, the Second Mate came running aft, singing out to know what was the matter. Then, suddenly, crouching under the rail near the log-reel, I saw something that looked like a man; but so hazy and unreal, that I could scarcely say I saw anything. Yet, like a flash, my thoughts ripped back to the silent figure I had seen in the flicker of the moonlight, a week earlier.

The Second Mate reached me, and I pointed, dumbly; and yet, as I did so, it was with the knowledge that he would not be able to see what I saw. (Queer, wasn't it?) And then, almost in a breath, I lost sight of the thing, and became aware that Tammy was hugging my knees.

The Second continued to stare at the log-reel for a brief instant; then he turned to me, with a sneer.

"Been asleep, the pair of you, I suppose!" Then, without waiting for my denial, he told Tammy to go to hell out of it and stop his noise, or he'd boot him off the poop.

After that, he walked forward to the break of the poop, and lit his pipe, again—walking forward and aft every few minutes, and eyeing me, at times, I thought, with a strange, half-doubtful, half-puzzled look.

Later, as soon as I was relieved, I hurried down to the 'Prentice's berth. I was anxious to speak to Tammy. There were a dozen questions that worried me, and I was in doubt what I ought to do. I found him crouched on a sea-chest, his knees up to his chin, and his gaze fixed on the doorway, with a frightened stare. I put my head into the berth, and he gave a gasp; then he saw who it was, and his face relaxed something of its strained expression.

He said: "Come in," in a low voice, which he tried to steady; and I stepped over the wash-board, and sat down on a chest, facing him.

"What was it?" he asked; putting his feet down on to the deck, and leaning forward. "For God's sake, tell me what it was!"

His voice had risen, and I put up my hand to warn him.

"H'sh!" I said. "You'll wake the other fellows."

He repeated his question, but in a lower tone. I hesitated, before answering him. I felt, all at once, that it might be better to deny all knowledge—to say I hadn't seen anything unusual. I thought quickly, and made answer on the turn of the moment.

"What was what?" I said. "That's just the thing I've come to ask you. A pretty pair of fools you made of the two of us up on the poop just now, with your hysterical tomfoolery."

I concluded my remark in a tone of anger.

"I didn't!" he answered, in a passionate whisper. "You know I didn't. You know you saw it yourself. You pointed it out to the Second Mate. I saw you."

The little beggar was nearly crying between fear, and vexation at my assumed unbelief.

"Rot!" I replied. "You know jolly well you were sleeping in your time-keeping. You dreamed something and woke up suddenly. You were off your chump."

I was determined to reassure him, if possible; though, goodness! I wanted assurance myself. If he had known of that other thing, I had seen down on the maindeck, what then?

"I wasn't asleep, any more than you were," he said, bitterly. "And you know it. You're just fooling me. The ship's haunted."

"What!" I said, sharply.

"She's haunted," he said, again. "She's haunted."

"Who says so?" I inquired, in a tone of unbelief.

"I do! And you know it. Everybody knows it; but they don't more than half believe it ... I didn't, until tonight."

"Damned rot!" I answered. "That's all a blooming old shellback's yarn. She's no more haunted than I am."

"It's not damned rot," he replied, totally unconvinced. "And it's not an old shellback's yarn ... Why won't you say you saw it?" he cried, growing almost tearfully excited, and raising his voice again.

I warned him not to wake the sleepers.

"Why won't you say that you saw it?" he repeated.

I got up from the chest, and went towards the door.

"You're a young idiot!" I said. "And I should advise you not to go gassing about like this, round the decks. Take my tip, and turn-in and get a sleep. You're talking dotty. Tomorrow you'll perhaps feel what an unholy ass you've made of yourself."

I stepped over the washboard, and left him. I believe he followed me to the door to say something further; but I was half-way forward by then.

For the next couple of days, I avoided him as much as possible, taking care never to let him catch me alone. I was determined, if possible, to convince him that he had been mistaken in supposing that he had seen anything that night. Yet, after all, it was little enough use, as you will soon see. For, on the night of the second day, there was a further extraordinary development, that made denial on my part useless.

THE MAN UP THE MAIN

It occurred in the first watch, just after six bells. I was forward, sitting on the fore-hatch. No one was about the maindeck. The night was exceedingly fine; and the wind had dropped away almost to nothing, so that the ship was very quiet.

Suddenly, I heard the Second Mate's voice—

"In the main-rigging, there! Who's that going aloft?"

I sat up on the hatch, and listened. There succeeded an intense silence. Then the Second's voice came again. He was evidently getting wild.

"Do you damn well hear me? What the hell are you doing up there? Come down!"

I rose to my feet, and walked up to wind'ard. From there, I could see the break of the poop. The Second Mate was standing by the starboard ladder. He appeared to be looking up at something that was hidden from me by the topsails. As I stared, he broke out again:

"Hell and damnation, you blasted sojer, come down when I tell you!"

He stamped on the poop, and repeated his order, savagely. But there was no answer. I started to walk aft. What had happened? Who had gone aloft? Who would be fool enough to go, without being told? And then, all at once, a thought came to me. The figure Tammy and I had seen. Had the Second Mate seen something—someone? I hurried on, and then stopped, suddenly. In the same moment there came the shrill blast of the Second's whistle; he was whistling for the watch, and I turned and ran to the fo'cas'le to rouse them out. Another minute, and I was hurrying aft with them to see what was wanted.

His voice met us half-way:

"Up the main some of you, smartly now, and find out who that damned fool is up there. See what mischief he's up to."

"i, i, Sir," several of the men sung out, and a couple jumped into the weather rigging. I joined them, and the rest were proceeding to follow; but the Second shouted for some to go up to leeward—in case the fellow tried to get down that side.

As I followed the other two aloft, I heard the Second Mate tell Tammy, whose time-keeping it was, to get down on to the maindeck with the other 'prentice, and keep an eye on the fore and aft stays.

"He may try down one of them if he's cornered," I heard him explain. "If you see anything, just sing out for me, right away."

Tammy hesitated.

"Well?" said the Second Mate, sharply.

"Nothing, Sir," said Tammy, and went down on to the maindeck.

The first man to wind'ard had reached the futtock shrouds; his head was above the top, and he was taking a preliminary look, before venturing higher.

"See anythin', Jock?" asked Plummer, the man next above me.

"Na'!" said Jock, tersely, and climbed over the top, and so disappeared from my sight.

The fellow ahead of me, followed. He reached the futtock rigging, and stopped to expectorate. I was close at his heels, and he looked down to me.

"What's up, anyway?" he said. "What's 'e seen? 'oo're we chasin' after?"

I said I didn't know, and he swung up into the topmast rigging. I followed on. The chaps on the lee side were about level with us. Under the foot of the topsail, I could see Tammy and the other 'prentice down on the maindeck, looking upwards.

The fellows were a bit excited in a sort of subdued way; though I am inclined to think there was far more curiosity and, perhaps, a certain consciousness of the strangeness of it all. I know that, looking to leeward, there was a tendancy to keep well together, in which I sympathised.

"Must be a bloomin' stowaway," one of the men suggested.

I grabbed at the idea, instantly. Perhaps—And then, in a moment, I dismissed it. I remembered how that first thing had stepped over the rail into the sea. That matter could not be explained in such a manner. With regard to this, I was curious and anxious. I had seen nothing this time. What could the Second Mate have seen? I wondered. Were we chasing fancies, or was there really someone—something real, among the shadows above us? My thoughts returned to that thing, Tammy and I had seen near the log-reel. I remembered how incapable the Second Mate had been of seeing anything then. I remembered how natural it had seemed that he should not be able to see. I caught the word "stowaway" again. After all, that might explain away this affair. It would—

My train of thought was broken suddenly. One of the men was shouting and gesticulating.

"I sees 'im! I sees 'im!" He was pointing upwards over our heads.

"Where?" said the man above me. "Where?"

I was looking up, for all that I was worth. I was conscious of a certain sense of relief. "It is real then," I said to myself. I screwed my head round, and looked along the yards above us. Yet, still I could see nothing; nothing except shadows and patches of light.

Down on deck, I caught the Second Mate's voice.

"Have you got him?" he was shouting.

"Not yet, Zur," sung out the lowest man on the lee side.

"We sees 'im, Sir," added Quoin.

"I don't!" I said.

"There 'e is agen," he said.

We had reached the t'gallant rigging, and he was pointing up to the royal yard.

"Ye're a fule, Quoin. That's what ye are."

The voice came from above. It was Jock's, and there was a burst of laughter at Quoin's expense.

I could see Jock now. He was standing in the rigging, just below the yard. He had gone straight away up, while the rest of us were mooning over the top.

"Ye're a fule, Quoin," he said, again, "And I'm thinking the Second's juist as saft."

He began to descend.

"Then there's no one?" I asked.

"Na'," he said, briefly.

As we reached the deck, the Second Mate ran down off the poop. He came towards us, with an expectant air.

"You've got him?" he asked, confidently.

"There wasn't anyone," I said.

"What!" he nearly shouted. "You're hiding something!" he continued, angrily, and glancing from one to another. "Out with it. Who was it?"

"We're hiding nothing," I replied, speaking for the lot. "There's no one up there."

The Second looked round upon us.

"Am I a fool?" he asked, contemptuously.

There was an assenting silence.

"I saw him myself," he continued. "Tammy, here, saw him. He wasn't over the top when I first spotted him. There's no mistake about it. It's all damned rot saying he's not there."

"Well, he's not, Sir," I answered. "Jock went right up to the royal yard."

The Second Mate said nothing, in immediate reply; but went aft a few steps and looked up the main. Then he turned to the two 'prentices.

"Sure you two boys didn't see anyone coming down from the main?" he inquired, suspiciously.

"Yes, Sir," they answered together.

"Anyway," I heard him mutter to himself, "I'd have spotted him myself, if he had."

"Have you any idea, Sir, who it was you saw?" I asked, at this juncture.

He looked at me, keenly.

"No!" he said.

He thought for a few moments, while we all stood about in silence, waiting for him to let us go.

"By the holy poker!" he exclaimed, suddenly. "But I ought to have thought of that before."

He turned, and eyed us individually.

"You're all here?" he asked.

"Yes, Sir," we said in a chorus. I could see that he was counting us. Then he spoke again.

"All of you men stay here where you are. Tammy, you go into your place and see if the other fellows are in their bunks. Then come and tell me. Smartly now!"

The boy went, and he turned to the other 'prentice.

"You get along forrard to the fo'cas'le," he said. "Count the other watch; then come aft and report to me."

As the youngster disappeared along the deck to the fo'cas'le, Tammy returned from his visit to the Glory Hole, to tell the Second Mate that the other two 'prentices were sound asleep in their bunks. Whereupon, the Second bundled him off to the Carpenter's and Sailmaker's berth, to see whether they were turned-in.

While he was gone, the other boy came aft, and reported that all the men were in their bunks, and asleep.

"Sure?" the Second asked him.

"Quite, Sir," he answered.

The Second Mate made a quick gesture.

"Go and see if the Steward is in his berth," he said, abruptly. It was plain to me that he was tremendously puzzled.

"You've something to learn yet, Mr. Second Mate," I thought to myself. Then I fell to wondering to what conclusions he would come.

A few seconds later, Tammy returned to say that the Carpenter, Sailmaker and "Doctor" were all turned-in.

The Second Mate muttered something, and told him to go down into the saloon to see whether the First and Third Mates, by any chance, were not in their berths.

Tammy started off; then halted.

"Shall I have a look into the Old Man's place, Sir, while I'm down there?" he inquired.

"No!" said the Second Mate. "Do what I told you, and then come and tell me. If anyone's to go into the Captain's cabin, it's got to be me."

Tammy said "i, i, Sir," and skipped away, up on to the poop.

While he was gone, the other 'prentice came up to say that the Steward was in his berth, and that he wanted to know what the hell he was fooling round his part of the ship for.

The Second Mate said nothing, for nearly a minute. Then he turned to us, and told us we might go forrard.

As we moved off in a body, and talking in undertones, Tammy came down from the poop, and went up to the Second Mate. I heard him say that the two Mates were in their berths, asleep. Then he added, as if it were an afterthought—

"So's the Old Man."

"I thought I told you—" the Second Mate began.

"I didn't, Sir," Tammy said. "His cabin door was open."

The Second Mate started to go aft. I caught a fragment of a remark he was making to Tammy.

"—accounted for the whole crew. I'm—"

He went up on to the poop. I did not catch the rest.

I had loitered a moment; now, however, I hurried after the others. As we neared the fo'cas'le, one bell went, and we roused out the other watch, and told them what jinks we had been up to.

"I rec'on 'e must be rocky," one of the men remarked.

"Not 'im," said another, "'e's bin 'avin' forty winks on the break, an' dreemed 'is mother-en-lore 'ad come on 'er visit, friendly like."

There was some laughter at this suggestion, and I caught myself smiling along with the rest; though I had no reason for sharing their belief, that there was nothing in it all.

"Might 'ave been a stowaway, yer know," I heard Quoin, the one who had suggested it before, remark to one of the A.B's named Stubbins—a short, rather surly-looking chap.

"Might have been hell!" returned Stubbins. "Stowaways hain't such fools as all that."

"I dunno," said the first. "I wish I 'ad arsked the Second what 'e thought about it."

"I don't think it was a stowaway, somehow," I said, chipping in. "What would a stowaway want aloft? I guess he'd be trying more for the Steward's pantry."

"You bet he would, hevry time," said Stubbins. He lit his pipe, and sucked at it, slowly.

"I don't hunderstand it, all ther same," he remarked, after a moment's silence.

"Neither do I," I said. And after that I was quiet for a while, listening to the run of conversation on the subject.

Presently, my glance fell upon Williams, the man who had spoken to me about "shadders." He was sitting in his bunk, smoking, and making no effort to join in the talk.

I went across to him.

"What do you think of it, Williams?" I asked. "Do you think the Second Mate really saw anything?"

He looked at me, with a sort of gloomy suspicion; but said nothing.

I felt a trifle annoyed by his silence; but took care not to show it. After a few moments, I went on.

"Do you know, Williams, I'm beginning to understand what you meant that night, when you said there were too many shadows."

"Wot yer mean?" he said, pulling his pipe from out of his mouth, and fairly surprised into answering.

"What I say, of course," I said. "There are too many shadows."

He sat up, and leant forward out from his bunk, extending his hand and pipe. His eyes plainly showed his excitement.

"'ave yer seen—" he hesitated, and looked at me, struggling inwardly to express himself.

"Well?" I prompted.

For perhaps a minute he tried to say something. Then his expression altered suddenly from doubt, and something else more indefinite, to a pretty grim look of determination.

He spoke.

"I'm blimed," he said, "ef I don't tike er piy-diy out of 'er, shadders or no shadders."

I looked at him, with astonishment.

"What's it got to do with your getting a pay-day out of her?" I asked.

He nodded his head, with a sort of stolid resolution.

"Look 'ere," he said.

I waited.

"Ther crowd cleared"; he indicated with his hand and pipe towards the stern.

"You mean in 'Frisco?" I said.

"Yus," he replied; "'an withart er cent of ther piy. I styied."

I comprehended him suddenly.

"You think they saw," I hesitated; then I said "shadows?"

He nodded; but said nothing.

"And so they all bunked?"

He nodded again, and began tapping out his pipe on the edge of his bunk-board.

"And the officers and the Skipper?" I asked.

"Fresh uns," he said, and got out of his bunk; for eight bells was striking.

The Fooling with the Sail

It was on the Friday night, that the Second Mate had the watch aloft looking for the man up the main; and for the next five days little else was talked about; though, with the exception of Williams, Tammy and myself, no one seemed to think of treating the matter seriously. Perhaps I should not exclude Quoin, who still persisted, on every occasion, that there was a stowaway aboard. As for the Second Mate, I have very little doubt now, but that he was beginning to realise there was something deeper and less understandable than he had at first dreamed of. Yet, all the same, I know he had to keep his guesses and half-formed opinions pretty well to himself; for the Old Man and the First Mate chaffed him unmercifully about his "bogy." This, I got from Tammy, who had heard them both ragging him during the second dog-watch the following day. There was another thing Tammy told me, that showed how the Second Mate bothered about his inability to understand the mysterious appearance and disappearance of the man he had seen go aloft. He had made Tammy give him every detail he could remember about the figure we had seen by the log-reel. What is more, the Second had not even affected to treat the matter lightly, nor as a thing to be sneered at; but had listened seriously, and asked a great many questions. It is very evident to me that he was reaching out towards the only possible conclusion. Though, goodness knows, it was one that was impossible and improbable enough.

It was on the Wednesday night, after the five days of talk I have mentioned, that there came, to me and to those who knew, another element of fear. And yet, I can quite understand that, at that time, those who had seen nothing, would find little to be afraid of, in all that I am going to tell you. Still, even they were much puzzled and astonished, and perhaps, after all, a little awed. There was so much in the affair that was inexplicable, and yet again such a lot that was natural and commonplace. For, when all is said and done, it was nothing more than the blowing adrift of one of the sails; yet accompanied by what were really significant details—significant, that is, in the light of that which Tammy and I and the Second Mate knew.

Seven bells, and then one, had gone in the first watch, and our side was being roused out to relieve the Mate's. Most of the men were already out of their bunks, and sitting about on their sea-chests, getting into their togs.

Suddenly, one of the 'prentices in the other watch, put his head in through the doorway on the port side.

"The Mate wants to know," he said, "which of you chaps made fast the fore royal, last watch."

"Wot's 'e want to know that for?" inquired one of the men.

"The lee side's blowing adrift," said the 'prentice. "And he says that the chap who made it fast is to go up and see to it as soon as the watch is relieved."

"Oh! does 'e? Well 'twasn't me, any'ow," replied the man. "You'd better arsk sum of t'others."

"Ask what?" inquired Plummer, getting out of his bunk, sleepily.

The 'prentice repeated his message.

The man yawned and stretched himself.

"Let me see," he muttered, and scratched his head with one hand, while he fumbled for his trousers with the other. "'oo made ther fore r'yal fast?" He got into his trousers, and stood up. "Why, ther Or'nary, er course; 'oo else do yer suppose?"

"That's all I wanted to know!" said the 'prentice, and went away.

"Hi! Tom!" Stubbins sung out to the Ordinary. "Wake up, you lazy young devil. Ther Mate's just sent to hinquire who it was made the fore royal fast. It's all blowin' adrift, and he says you're to get along up as soon as eight bells goes, and make it fast again."

Tom jumped out of his bunk, and began to dress, quickly.

"Blowin' adrift!" he said. "There ain't all that much wind; and I tucked the ends of the gaskets well in under the other turns."

"P'raps one of ther gaskets is rotten, and given way," suggested Stubbins. "Anyway, you'd better hurry up, it's just on eight bells."

A minute later, eight bells went, and we trooped away aft for roll-call. As soon as the names were called over, I saw the Mate lean towards the Second and say something. Then the Second Mate sung out:

"Tom!"

"Sir!" answered Tom.

"Was it you made fast that fore royal, last watch?"

"Yes, Sir."

"How's that it's broken adrift?"

"Carn't say, Sir."

"Well, it has, and you'd better jump aloft and shove the gasket round it again. And mind you make a better job of it this time."

"i, i, Sir," said Tom, and followed the rest of us forrard. Reaching the fore rigging, he climbed into it, and began to make his way leisurely aloft. I could see him with a fair amount of distinctness, as the moon was very clear and bright, though getting old.

I went over to the weather pin-rail, and leaned up against it, watching him, while I filled my pipe. The other men, both the watch on deck and the watch below, had gone into the fo'cas'le, so that I imagined I was the only one about the maindeck. Yet, a minute later, I discovered that I was mistaken; for, as I proceeded to light up, I saw Williams, the young cockney, come out from under the lee of the house, and turn and look up at the Ordinary as he went steadily upwards. I was a little surprised, as I knew he and three of the others had a "poker fight" on, and he'd won over sixty pounds of tobacco. I believe I opened my mouth to sing out to him to know why he wasn't playing; and then, all at once, there came into my mind the memory of my first conversation with him. I remembered that he had said sails were always blowing adrift at night. I remembered the, then, unaccountable emphasis he had laid on those two words; and remembering that, I felt suddenly afraid. For, all at once, the absurdity had struck me of a sail—even a badly stowed one—blowing adrift in such fine and calm weather as we were then having. I wondered I had not seen before that there was something queer and unlikely about the affair. Sails don't blow adrift in fine weather, with the sea calm and the ship as steady as a rock. I moved away from the rail and went towards Williams. He knew something, or, at least, he guessed at something that was very much a blankness to me at that time. Up above, the boy was climbing up, to what? That was the thing that made me feel so frightened. Ought I to tell all I knew and guessed? And then, who should I tell? I should only be laughed at—I—

Williams turned towards me, and spoke.

"Gawd!" he said, "it's started agen!"

"What?" I said. Though I knew what he meant.

"Them syles," he answered, and made a gesture towards the fore royal.

I glanced up, briefly. All the lee side of the sail was adrift, from the bunt gasket outwards. Lower, I saw Tom; he was just hoisting himself into the t'gallant rigging.

Williams spoke again.

"We lost two on 'em just sime way, comin' art."

"Two of the men!" I exclaimed.

"Yus!" he said tersely.

"I can't understand," I went on. "I never heard anything about it."

"Who'd yer got ter tell yer abart it?" he asked.

I made no reply to his question; indeed, I had scarcely comprehended it, for the problem of what I ought to do in the matter had risen again in my mind.

"I've a good mind to go aft and tell the Second Mate all I know," I said. "He's seen something himself that he can't explain away, and—and anyway I can't stand this state of things. If the Second Mate knew all—"

"Garn!" he cut in, interrupting me. "An' be told yer're a blastid hidiot. Not yer. Yer sty were yer are."

I stood irresolute. What he had said, was perfectly correct, and I was positively stumped what to do for the best. That there was danger aloft, I was convinced; though if I had been asked my reasons for supposing this, they would have been hard to find. Yet of its existence, I was as certain as though my eyes already saw it. I wondered whether, being so ignorant of the form it would assume, I could stop it by joining Tom on the yard? This thought came as I stared up at the royal. Tom had reached the sail, and was standing on the foot-rope, close in to the bunt. He was bending over the yard, and reaching down for the slack of the sail. And then, as I looked, I saw the belly of the royal tossed up and down abruptly, as though a sudden heavy gust of wind had caught it.

"I'm blimed—!" Williams began, with a sort of excited expectation. And then he stopped as abruptly as he had begun. For, in a moment, the sail had thrashed right over the after side of the yard, apparently knocking Tom clean from off the foot-rope.

"My God!" I shouted out loud. "He's gone!"

For an instant there was a blur over my eyes, and Williams was singing out something that I could not catch. Then, just as quickly, it went, and I could see again, clearly.

Williams was pointing, and I saw something black, swinging below the yard. Williams called out something fresh, and made a run for the fore rigging. I caught the last part—

"—ther garskit."

Straightway, I knew that Tom had managed to grab the gasket as he fell, and I bolted after Williams to give him a hand in getting the youngster into safety.

Down on deck, I caught the sound of running feet, and then the Second Mate's voice. He was asking what the devil was up; but I did not trouble to answer him then. I wanted all my breath to help me aloft. I knew very well that some of the gaskets were little better than old shakins; and, unless Tom got hold of something on the t'gallant yard below him, he might come down with a run any moment. I reached the top, and lifted myself over it in quick time. Williams was some distance above me. In less than half a minute, I reached the t'gallant yard. Williams had gone up on to the royal. I slid out on to the t'gallant foot-rope until I was just below Tom; then I sung out to him to let himself down to me, and I would catch him. He made no answer, and I saw that he was hanging in a curiously limp fashion, and by one hand.

Williams's voice came down to me from the royal yard. He was singing out to me to go up and give him a hand to pull Tom up on to the yard. When I reached him, he told me that the gasket had hitched itself round the lad's wrist. I bent beside the yard, and peered down. It was as Williams had said, and I realised how near a thing it had been. Strangely enough, even at that moment, the thought came to me how little wind there was. I remembered the wild way in which the sail had lashed at the boy.

All this time, I was busily working, unreeving the port buntline. I took the end, made a running bowline with it round the gasket, and let the loop slide down over the boy's head and shoulders. Then I took a strain on it and tightened it under his arms. A minute later we had him safely on the yard between us. In the uncertain moonlight, I could just make out the mark of a great lump on his forehead, where the foot of the sail must have caught him when it knocked him over.

As we stood there a moment, taking our breath, I caught the sound of the Second Mate's voice close beneath us. Williams glanced down; then he looked up at me and gave a short, grunting laugh.

"Crikey!" he said.

"What's up?" I asked, quickly.

He jerked his head backwards and downwards. I screwed round a bit, holding the jackstay with one hand, and steadying the insensible Ordinary with the other. In this way I could look below. At first, I could see nothing. Then the Second Mate's voice came up to me again.

"Who the hell are you? What are you doing?"

I saw him now. He was standing at the foot of the weather t'gallant rigging, his face was turned upwards, peering round the after side of the mast. It showed to me only as a blurred, pale-coloured oval in the moonlight.

He repeated his question.

"It's Williams and I, Sir," I said. "Tom, here, has had an accident."

I stopped. He began to come up higher towards us. From the rigging to leeward there came suddenly a buzz of men talking.

The Second Mate reached us.

"Well, what's up, anyway?" he inquired, suspiciously. "What's happened?"

He had bent forward, and was peering at Tom. I started to explain; but he cut me short with:

"Is he dead?"

"No, Sir," I said. "I don't think so; but the poor beggar's had a bad fall. He was hanging by the gasket when we got to him. The sail knocked him off the yard."

"What?" he said, sharply.

"The wind caught the sail, and it lashed back over the yard—"

"What wind?" he interrupted. "There's no wind, scarcely." He shifted his weight on to the other foot. "What do you mean?"

"I mean what I say, Sir. The wind brought the foot of the sail over the top of the yard and knocked Tom clean off the foot-rope. Williams and I both saw it happen."

"But there's no wind to do such a thing; you're talking nonsense!"

It seemed to me that there was as much of bewilderment as anything else in his voice; yet I could tell that he was suspicious—though, of what, I doubted whether he himself could have told.

He glanced at Williams, and seemed about to say something. Then, seeming to change his mind, he turned, and sung out to one of the men who had followed him aloft, to go down and pass out a coil of new, three-inch manilla, and a tailblock.

"Smartly now!" he concluded.

"i, i, Sir," said the man, and went down swiftly.

The Second Mate turned to me.

"When you've got Tom below, I shall want a better explanation of all this, than the one you've given me. It won't wash."

"Very well, Sir," I answered. "But you won't get any other."

"What do you mean?" he shouted at me. "I'll let you know I'll have no impertinence from you or any one else."

"I don't mean any impertinence, Sir—I mean that it's the only explanation there is to give."

"I tell you it won't wash!" he repeated. "There's something too damned funny about it all. I shall have to report the matter to the Captain. I can't tell him that yarn—" He broke off abruptly.

"It's not the only damned funny thing that's happened aboard this old hooker," I answered. "You ought to know that, Sir."

"What do you mean?" he asked, quickly.

"Well, Sir," I said, "to be straight, what about that chap you sent us hunting after up the main the other night? That was a funny enough affair, wasn't it? This one isn't half so funny."

"That will do, Jessop!" he said, angrily. "I won't have any back talk." Yet there was something about his tone that told me I had got one in on my own. He seemed all at once less able to appear confident that I was telling him a fairy tale.

After that, for perhaps half a minute, he said nothing. I guessed he was doing some hard thinking. When he spoke again it was on the matter of getting the Ordinary down on deck.

"One of you'll have to go down the lee side and steady him down," he concluded.

He turned and looked downwards.

"Are you bringing that gantline?" he sang out.

"Yes, Sir," I heard one of the men answer.

A moment later, I saw the man's head appear over the top. He had the tail-block slung round his neck, and the end of the gantline over his shoulder.

Very soon we had the gantline rigged, and Tom down on deck. Then we took him into the fo'cas'le and put him in his bunk. The Second Mate had sent for some brandy, and now he started to dose him well with it. At the same time a couple of the men chafed his hands and feet. In a little, he began to show signs of coming round. Presently, after a sudden fit of coughing, he opened his eyes, with a surprised, bewildered stare. Then he caught at the edge of his bunk-board, and sat up, giddily. One of the men steadied him, while the Second Mate stood back, and eyed him, critically. The boy rocked as he sat, and put up his hand to his head.

"Here," said the Second Mate, "take another drink."

Tom caught his breath and choked a little; then he spoke.

"By gum!" he said, "my head does ache."

He put up his hand, again, and felt at the lump on his forehead. Then he bent forward and stared round at the men grouped about his bunk.

"What's up?" he inquired, in a confused sort of way, and seeming as if he could not see us clearly.

"What's up?" he asked again.

"That's just what I want to know!" said the Second Mate, speaking for the first time with some sternness.

"I ain't been snoozin' while there's been a job on?" Tom inquired, anxiously.

He looked round at the men appealingly.

"It's knocked 'im dotty, strikes me," said one of the men, audibly.

"No," I said, answering Tom's question, "you've had—"

"Shut that, Jessop!" said the Second Mate, quickly, interrupting me. "I want to hear what the boy's got to say for himself."

He turned again to Tom.

"You were up at the fore royal," he prompted.

"I carn't say I was, Sir," said Tom, doubtfully. I could see that he had not gripped the Second Mate's meaning.

"But you were!" said the Second, with some impatience. "It was blowing adrift, and I sent you up to shove a gasket round it."

"Blowin' adrift, Sir?" said Tom, dully.

"Yes! blowing adrift. Don't I speak plainly?"

The dullness went from Tom's face, suddenly.

"So it was, Sir," he said, his memory returning. "The bloomin' sail got chock full of wind. It caught me bang in the face."

He paused a moment.

"I believe—" he began, and then stopped once more.

"Go on!" said the Second Mate. "Spit it out!"

"I don't know, Sir," Tom said. "I don't understand—"

He hesitated again.

"That's all I can remember," he muttered, and put his hand up to the bruise on his forehead, as though trying to remember something.

In the momentary silence that succeeded, I caught the voice of Stubbins.

"There hain't hardly no wind," he was saying, in a puzzled tone.

There was a low murmur of assent from the surrounding men.

The Second Mate said nothing, and I glanced at him, curiously. Was he beginning to see, I wondered, how useless it was to try to find any sensible explanation of the affair? Had he begun at last to couple it with that peculiar business of the man up the main? I am inclined now to think that this was so; for, after staring a few moments at Tom, in a doubtful sort of way, he went out of the fo'cas'le, saying that he would inquire further into the matter in the morning. Yet, when the morning came, he did no such thing. As for his reporting the affair to the Skipper, I much doubt it. Even did he, it must have been in a very casual way; for we heard nothing more about it; though, of course, we talked it over pretty thoroughly among ourselves.

With regard to the Second Mate, even now I am rather puzzled by his attitude to us aloft. Sometimes I have thought that he must have suspected us of trying to play off some trick on him—perhaps, at the time, he still half suspected one of us of being in some way connected with the other business. Or, again, he may have been trying to fight against the conviction that was being forced upon him, that there was really something impossible and beastly about the old packet. Of course, these are only suppositions.

And then, close upon this, there were further developments.

The End of Williams

As I have said, there was a lot of talk, among the crowd of us forrard, about Tom's strange accident. None of the men knew that Williams and I had seen it happen. Stubbins gave it as his opinion that Tom had been sleepy, and missed the foot-rope. Tom, of course, would not have this by any means. Yet, he had no one to appeal to; for, at that time, he was just as ignorant as the rest, that we had seen the sail flap up over the yard.

Stubbins insisted that it stood to reason it couldn't be the wind. There wasn't any, he said; and the rest of the men agreed with him.

"Well," I said, "I don't know about all that. I'm a bit inclined to think Tom's yarn is the truth."

"How do you make that hout?" Stubbins asked, unbelievingly. "There haint nothin' like enough wind."

"What about the place on his forehead?" I inquired, in turn. "How are you going to explain that?"

"I 'spect he knocked himself there when he slipped," he answered.

"Likely 'nuffli," agreed old Jaskett, who was sitting smoking on a chest near by.

"Well, you're both a damn long way out of it!" Tom chipped in, pretty warm. "I wasn't asleep; an' the sail did bloomin' well hit me."

"Don't you be impertinent, young feller," said Jaskett.

I joined in again.

"There's another thing, Stubbins," I said. "The gasket Tom was hanging by, was on the after side of the yard. That looks as if the sail might have flapped it over? If there were wind enough to do the one, it seems to me that it might have done the other."

"Do you mean that it was hunder ther yard, or hover ther top?" he asked.

"Over the top, of course. What's more, the foot of the sail was hanging over the after part of the yard, in a bight."

Stubbins was plainly surprised at that, and before he was ready with his next objection, Plummer spoke.

"'oo saw it?" he asked.

"I saw it!" I said, a bit sharply. "So did Williams; so—for that matter—did the Second Mate."

Plummer relapsed into silence; and smoked; and Stubbins broke out afresh.

"I reckon Tom must have had a hold of the foot and the gasket, and pulled 'em hover the yard when he tumbled."

"No!" interrupted Tom. "The gasket was under the sail. I couldn't even see it. An' I hadn't time to get hold of the foot of the sail, before it up and caught me smack in the face."

"'ow did yer get 'old er ther gasket, when yer fell, then?" asked Plummer.

"He didn't get hold of it," I answered for Tom. "It had taken a turn round his wrist, and that's how we found him hanging."

"Do you mean to say as 'e 'adn't got 'old of ther garsket?," Quoin inquired, pausing in the lighting of his pipe.

"Of course, I do," I said. "A chap doesn't go hanging on to a rope when he's jolly well been knocked senseless."

"Ye're richt," assented Jock. "Ye're quite richt there, Jessop."

Quoin concluded the lighting of his pipe.

"I dunno," he said.

I went on, without noticing him.

"Anyway, when Williams and I found him, he was hanging by the gasket, and it had a couple of turns round his wrist. And besides that, as I said before, the foot of the sail was hanging over the after side of the yard, and Tom's weight on the gasket was holding it there."

"It's damned queer," said Stubbins, in a puzzled voice. "There don't seem to be no way of gettin' a proper hexplanation to it."

I glanced at Williams, to suggest that I should tell all that we had seen; but he shook his head, and, after a moment's thought, it seemed to me that there was nothing to be gained by so doing. We had no very clear idea of the thing that had happened, and our half facts and guesses would only have tended to make the matter appear more grotesque and unlikely. The only thing to be done was to wait and watch. If we could only get hold of something tangible, then we might hope to tell all that we knew, without being made into laughing-stocks.

I came out from my think, abruptly.

Stubbins was speaking again. He was arguing the matter with one of the other men.

"You see, with there bein' no wind, scarcely, ther thing's himpossible, an' yet—"

The other man interrupted with some remark I did not catch.

"No," I heard Stubbins say. "I'm hout of my reckonin'. I don't savvy it one bit. It's too much like a damned fairy tale."

"Look at his wrist!" I said.

Tom held out his right hand and arm for inspection. It was considerably swollen where the rope had been round it.

"Yes," admitted Stubbins. "That's right enough; but it don't tell you nothin'."

I made no reply. As Stubbins said, it told you "nothin'." And there I let it drop. Yet, I have told you this, as showing how the matter was regarded in the fo'cas'le. Still, it did not occupy our minds very long; for, as I have said, there were further developments.

The three following nights passed quietly; and then, on the fourth, all those curious signs and hints culminated suddenly in something extraordinarily grim. Yet, everything had been so subtle and intangible, and, indeed, so was the affair itself, that only those who had actually come in touch with the invading fear, seemed really capable of comprehending the terror of the thing. The men, for the most part, began to say the ship was unlucky, and, of course, as usual! there was some talk of there being a Jonah in the ship. Still, I cannot say that none of the men realised there was anything horrible and frightening in it all; for I am sure that some did, a little; and I think Stubbins was certainly one of them; though I feel certain that he did not, at that time, you know, grasp a quarter of the real significance that underlay the several queer matters that had disturbed our nights. He seemed to fail, somehow, to grasp the element of personal danger that, to me, was already plain. He lacked sufficient imagination, I suppose, to piece the things together—to trace the natural sequence of the events, and their development. Yet I must not forget, of course, that he had no knowledge of those two first incidents. If he had, perhaps he might have stood where I did. As it was, he had not seemed to reach out at all, you know, not even in the matter of Tom and the fore royal. Now, however, after the thing I am about to tell you, he seemed to see a little way into the darkness, and realise possibilities.

I remember the fourth night, well. It was a clear, star-lit, moonless sort of night: at least, I think there was no moon; or, at any rate, the moon could have been little more than a thin crescent, for it was near the dark time.

The wind had breezed up a bit; but still remained steady. We were slipping along at about six or seven knots an hour. It was our middle watch on deck, and the ship was full of the blow and hum of the wind aloft.

Williams and I were the only ones about the maindeck. He was leaning over the weather pin-rail, smoking; while I was pacing up and down, between him and the fore hatch. Stubbins was on the look-out.

Two bells had gone some minutes, and I was wishing to goodness that it was eight, and time to turn-in. Suddenly, overhead, there sounded a sharp crack, like the report of a rifle shot. It was followed instantly by the rattle and crash of sailcloth thrashing in the wind.

Williams jumped away from the rail, and ran aft a few steps. I followed him, and, together, we stared upwards to see what had gone. Indistinctly, I made out that the weather sheet of the fore t'gallant had carried away, and the clew of the sail was whirling and banging about in the air, and, every few moments, hitting the steel yard a blow, like the thump of a great sledge hammer.

"It's the shackle, or one of the links that's gone, I think," I shouted to Williams, above the noise of the sail. "That's the spectacle that's hitting the yard."

"Yus!" he shouted back, and went to get hold of the clewline. I ran to give him a hand. At the same moment, I caught the Second Mate's voice away aft, shouting. Then came the noise of running feet, and the rest of the watch, and the Second Mate, were with us almost at the same moment. In a few minutes we had the yard lowered and the sail clewed up. Then Williams and I went aloft to see where the sheet had gone. It was much as I had supposed; the spectacle was all right, but the pin had gone out of the shackle, and the shackle itself was jammed into the sheavehole in the yard arm.

Williams sent me down for another pin, while he unbent the clewline, and overhauled it down to the sheet. When I returned with the fresh pin, I screwed it into the shackle, clipped on the clewline, and sung out to the men to take a pull on the rope. This they did, and at the second heave the shackle came away. When it was high enough, I went up on to the t'gallant yard, and held the chain, while Williams shackled it into the spectacle. Then he bent on the clewline afresh, and sung out to the Second Mate that we were ready to hoist away.

"Yer'd better go down an' give 'em a 'aul," he said. "I'll sty an' light up ther syle."

"Right ho, Williams," I said, getting into the rigging. "Don't let the ship's bogy run away with you."

This remark I made in a moment of light-heartedness, such as will come to anyone aloft, at times. I was exhilarated for the time being, and quite free from the sense of fear that had been with me so much of late. I suppose this was due to the freshness of the wind.

"There's more'n one!" he said, in that curiously short way of his.

"What?" I asked.

He repeated his remark.

I was suddenly serious. The reality of all the impossible details of the past weeks came back to me, vivid, and beastly.

"What do you mean, Williams?" I asked him.

But he had shut up, and would say nothing.

"What do you know—how much do you know?" I went on, quickly. "Why did you never tell me that you—"

The Second Mate's voice interrupted me, abruptly:

"Now then, up there! Are you going to keep us waiting all night? One of you come down and give us a pull with the ha'lyards. The other stay up and light up the gear."

"i, i, Sir," I shouted back.

Then I turned to Williams, hurriedly.

"Look here, Williams," I said. "If you think there is really a danger in your being alone up here—" I hesitated for words to express what I meant. Then I went on. "Well, I'll jolly well stay up with you."

The Second Mate's voice came again.

"Come on now, one of you! Make a move! What the hell are you doing?"

"Coming, Sir!" I sung out.

"Shall I stay?" I asked definitely.

"Garn!" he said. "Don't yer fret yerself. I'll tike er bloomin' piy-diy out of 'er. Blarst 'em. I ain't funky of 'em."

I went. That was the last word Williams spoke to anyone living.

I reached the decks, and tailed on to the haulyards.

We had nearly mast-headed the yard, and the Second Mate was looking up at the dark outline of the sail, ready to sing out "Belay"; when, all at once, there came a queer sort of muffled shout from Williams.

"Vast hauling, you men," shouted the Second Mate.

We stood silent, and listened.

"What's that, Williams?" he sung out. "Are you all clear?"

For nearly half a minute we stood, listening; but there came no reply. Some of the men said afterwards that they had noticed a curious rattling and vibrating noise aloft that sounded faintly above the hum and swirl of the wind. Like the sound of loose ropes being shaken and slatted together, you know. Whether this noise was really heard, or whether it was something that had no existence outside of their imaginations, I cannot say. I heard nothing of it; but then I was at the tail end of the rope, and furthest from the fore rigging; while those who heard it were on the fore part of the haulyards, and close up to the shrouds.

The Second Mate put his hands to his mouth.

"Are you all clear there?" he shouted again.

The answer came, unintelligible and unexpected. It ran like this:

"Blarst yer ... I've styed ... Did yer think ... drive ... bl—y piy-diy." And then there was a sudden silence.

I stared up at the dim sail, astonished.

"He's dotty!" said Stubbins, who had been told to come off the look-out and give us a pull.

"'e's as mad as a bloomin' 'atter," said Quoin, who was standing foreside of me. "'e's been queer all along."

"Silence there!" shouted the Second Mate. Then:

"Williams!"

No answer.

"Williams!" more loudly.

Still no answer.

Then:

"Damn you, you jumped-up cockney crocodile! Can't you hear? Are you blooming-well deaf?"

There was no answer, and the Second Mate turned to me.

"Jump aloft, smartly now, Jessop, and see what's wrong!"

"i, i, Sir," I said and made a run for the rigging. I felt a bit queer. Had Williams gone mad? He certainly always had been a bit funny. Or—and the thought came with a jump—had he seen—I did not finish. Suddenly, up aloft, there sounded a frightful scream. I stopped, with my hand on the sheerpole. The next instant, something fell out of the darkness—a heavy body, that struck the deck near the waiting men, with a tremendous crash and a loud, ringing, wheezy sound that sickened me. Several of the men shouted out loud in their fright, and let go of the haulyards; but luckily the stopper held it, and the yard did not come down. Then, for the space of several seconds, there was a dead silence among the crowd; and it seemed to me that the wind had in it a strange moaning note.

The Second Mate was the first to speak. His voice came so abruptly that it startled me.

"Get a light, one of you, quick now!"

There was a moment's hesitation.

"Fetch one of the binnacle lamps, you, Tammy."

"i, i, Sir," the youngster said, in a quavering voice, and ran aft.

In less than a minute I saw the light coming towards us along the deck. The boy was running. He reached us, and handed the lamp to the Second Mate, who took it and went towards the dark, huddled heap on the deck. He held the light out before him, and peered at the thing.

"My God!" he said. "It's Williams!"

He stooped lower with the light, and I saw details. It was Williams right enough. The Second Mate told a couple of the men to lift him and straighten him out on the hatch. Then he went aft to call the Skipper. He returned in a couple of minutes with an old ensign which he spread over the poor beggar. Almost directly, the Captain came hurrying forward along the decks. He pulled back one end of the ensign, and looked; then he put it back quietly, and the Second Mate explained all that we knew, in a few words.

"Would you leave him where he is, Sir?" he asked, after he had told everything.

"The night's fine," said the Captain. "You may as well leave the poor devil there."

He turned, and went aft, slowly. The man who was holding the light, swept it round so that it showed the place where Williams had struck the deck.

The Second Mate spoke abruptly.

"Get a broom and a couple of buckets, some of you."

He turned sharply, and ordered Tammy on to the poop.

As soon as he had seen the yard mast-headed, and the ropes cleared up, he followed Tammy. He knew well enough that it would not do for the youngster to let his mind dwell too much on the poor chap on the hatch, and I found out, a little later, that he gave the boy something to occupy his thoughts.

After they had gone aft, we went into the fo'cas'le. Every one was moody and frightened. For a little while, we sat about in our bunks and on the chests, and no one said a word. The watch below were all asleep, and not one of them knew what had happened.

All at once, Plummer, whose wheel it was, stepped over the starboard washboard, into the fo'cas'le.

"What's up, anyway?" he asked. "Is Williams much 'urt?"

"Sh!" I said. "You'll wake the others. Who's taken your wheel?"

"Tammy—ther Second sent 'im. 'e said I could go forrard an' 'ave er smoke. 'e said Williams 'ad 'ad er fall."

He broke off, and looked across the fo'cas'le.

"Where is 'e?" he inquired, in a puzzled voice.

I glanced at the others; but no one seemed inclined to start yarning about it.

"He fell from the t'gallant rigging!" I said.

"Where is 'e?" he repeated.

"Smashed up," I said. "He's lying on the hatch."

"Dead?" he asked.

I nodded.

"I guessed 'twere somethin' pretty bad, when I saw the Old Man come forrard. 'ow did it 'appen?"

He looked round at the lot of us sitting there silent and smoking.

"No one knows," I said, and glanced at Stubbins. I caught him eyeing me, doubtfully.

After a moment's silence, Plummer spoke again.

"I 'eard 'im screech, when I was at ther wheel. 'e must 'ave got 'urt up aloft."

Stubbins struck a match and proceeded to relight his pipe.

"How d'yer mean?" he asked, speaking for the first time.

"'ow do I mean? Well, I can't say. Maybe 'e jammed 'is fingers between ther parrel an' ther mast."

"What about 'is swearin' at ther Second Mate? Was that 'cause 'e'd jammed 'is fingers?" put in Quoin.

"I never 'eard about that," said Plummer. "'oo 'eard 'im?

"I should think heverybody in ther bloomin' ship heard him," Stubbins answered. "All ther same, I hain't sure he was swearin' at ther Second Mate. I thought at first he'd gone dotty an' was cussin' him; but somehow it don't seem likely, now I come to think. It don't stand to reason he should go to cuss ther man. There was nothin' to go cussin' about. What's more, he didn't seem ter be talkin' down to us on deck— what I could make hout. 'sides, what would he want ter go talkin' to ther Second about his pay-day?"

He looked across to where I was sitting. Jock, who was smoking, quietly, on the chest next to me, took his pipe slowly out from between his teeth.

"Ye're no far oot, Stubbins, I'm thinkin'. Ye're no far oot," he said, nodding his head.

Stubbins still continued to gaze at me.

"What's your idee?" he said, abruptly.

It may have been my fancy, but it seemed to me that there was something deeper than the mere sense the question conveyed.

I glanced at him. I couldn't have said, myself, just what my idea was.

"I don't know!" I answered, a little adrift. "He didn't strike me as cursing at the Second Mate. That is, I should say, after the first minute."

"Just what I say," he replied. "Another thing—don't it strike you as bein' bloomin' queer about Tom nearly comin' down by ther run, an' then this?"

I nodded.

"It would have been all hup with Tom, if it hadn't been for ther gasket."

He paused. After a moment, he went on again.

"That was honly three or four nights ago!"

"Well," said Plummer. "What are yer drivin' at?"

"Nothin'," answered Stubbins. "Honly it's damned queer. Looks as though ther ship might be unlucky, after all."

"Well," agreed Plummer. "Things 'as been a bit funny lately; and then there's what's 'appened ter-night. I shall 'ang on pretty tight ther next time I go aloft."

Old Jaskett took his pipe from his mouth, and sighed.

"Things is going wrong 'most every night," he said, almost pathetically. "It's as diff'rent as chalk 'n' cheese ter what it were w'en we started this 'ere trip. I thought it were all 'ellish rot about 'er bein' 'aunted; but it's not, seem'ly."

He stopped and expectorated.

"She hain't haunted," said Stubbins. "Leastways, not like you mean—"

He paused, as though trying to grasp some elusive thought.

"Eh?" said Jaskett, in the interval.

Stubbins continued, without noticing the query. He appeared to be answering some half-formed thought in his own brain, rather than Jaskett:

"Things is queer—an' it's been a bad job tonight. I don't savvy one bit what Williams was sayin' of hup aloft. I've thought sometimes he'd somethin' on 'is mind—"

Then, after a pause of about half a minute, he said this:

"Who was he sayin' that to?"

"Eh?" said Jaskett, again, with a puzzled expression.

"I was thinkin'," said Stubbins, knocking out his pipe on the edge of the chest. "P'raps you're right, hafter all."

Another Man to the Wheel

The conversation had slacked off. We were all moody and shaken, and I know I, for one, was thinking some rather troublesome thoughts.

Suddenly, I heard the sound of the Second's whistle. Then his voice came along the deck:

"Another man to the wheel!"

"'e's singin' out for some one to go aft an' relieve ther wheel," said Quoin, who had gone to the door to listen. "Yer'd better 'urry up, Plummer."

"What's ther time?" asked Plummer, standing up and knocking out his pipe. "Must be close on ter four bells, 'oo's next wheel is it?"

"It's all right, Plummer," I said, getting up from the chest on which I had been sitting. "I'll go along. It's my wheel, and it only wants a couple of minutes to four bells."

Plummer sat down again, and I went out of the fo'cas'le. Reaching the poop, I met Tammy on the lee side, pacing up and down.

"Who's at the wheel?" I asked him, in astonishment.

"The Second Mate," he said, in a shaky sort of voice. "He's waiting to be relieved. I'll tell you all about it as soon as I get a chance."

I went on aft to the wheel.

"Who's that?" the Second inquired.

"It's Jessop, Sir," I answered.

He gave me the course, and then, without another word, went forrard along the poop. On the break, I heard him call Tammy's name, and then for some minutes he was talking to him; though what he was saying, I could not possibly hear. For my part, I was tremendously curious to know why the Second Mate had taken the wheel. I knew that if it were just a matter of bad steering on Tammy's part, he would not have dreamt of doing such a thing. There had been something queer happening, about which I had yet to learn; of this, I felt sure.

Presently, the Second Mate left Tammy, and commenced to walk the weather side of the deck. Once he came right aft, and, stooping down, peered under the wheel-box; but never addressed a word to me. Sometime later, he went down the weather ladder on to the main-deck. Directly afterwards, Tammy came running up to the lee side of the wheel-box.

"I've seen it again!" he said, gasping with sheer nervousness.

"What?" I said.

"That thing," he answered. Then he leant across the wheel-box, and lowered his voice.

"It came over the lee rail—up out of the sea," he added, with an air of telling something unbelievable.

I turned more towards him; but it was too dark to see his face with any distinctness. I felt suddenly husky. "My God!" I thought. And then I made a silly effort to protest; but he cut me short with a certain impatient hopelessness.

"For God's sake, Jessop," he said, "do stow all that! It's no good. I must have someone to talk to, or I shall go dotty."

I saw how useless it was to pretend any sort of ignorance. Indeed, really, I had known it all along, and avoided the youngster on that very account, as you know.

"Go on," I said. "I'll listen; but you'd better keep an eye for the Second Mate; he may pop up any minute."

For a moment, he said nothing, and I saw him peering stealthily about the poop.

"Go on," I said. "You'd better make haste, or he'll be up before you're half-way through. What was he doing at the wheel when I came up to relieve it? Why did he send you away from it?"

"He didn't," Tammy replied, turning his face towards me. "I bunked away from it."

"What for?" I asked.

"Wait a minute," he answered, "and I'll tell you the whole business. You know the Second Mate sent me to the wheel, after that—" He nodded his head forrard.

"Yes," I said.

"Well, I'd been here about ten minutes, or a quarter of an hour, and I was feeling rotten about Williams, and trying to forget it all and keep the ship on her course, and all that; when, all at once, I happened to glance to loo'ard, and there I saw it climbing over the rail. My God! I didn't know what to do. The Second Mate was standing forrard on the break of the poop, and I was here all by myself. I felt as if I were frozen stiff. When it came towards me, I let go of the wheel, and yelled and bunked forrard to the Second Mate. He caught hold of me and shook me; but I was so jolly frightened, I couldn't say a word. I could only keep on pointing. The Second kept asking me 'Where?' And then, all at once, I found I couldn't see the thing. I don't know whether he saw it. I'm not at all certain he did.

He just told me to damn well get back to the wheel, and stop making a damned fool of myself. I said out straight I wouldn't go. So he blew his whistle, and sung out for someone to come aft and take it. Then he ran and got hold of the wheel himself. You know the rest."

"You're quite sure it wasn't thinking about Williams made you imagine you saw something?" I said, more to gain a moment to think, than because I believed that it was the case.

"I thought you were going to listen to me, seriously!" he said, bitterly. "If you won't believe me; what about the chap the Second Mate saw? What about Tom? What about Williams? For goodness sake! don't try to put me off like you did last time. I nearly went cracked with wanting to tell someone who would listen to me, and wouldn't laugh. I could stand anything, but this being alone. There's a good chap, don't pretend you don't understand. Tell me what it all means. What is this horrible man that I've twice seen? You know you know something, and I believe you're afraid to tell anyone, for fear of being laughed at. Why don't you tell me? You needn't be afraid of my laughing."

He stopped, suddenly. For the moment, I said nothing in reply.

"Don't treat me like a kid, Jessop!" he exclaimed, quite passionately.

"I won't," I said, with a sudden resolve to tell him everything. "I need someone to talk to, just as badly as you do."

"What does it all mean, then?" he burst out. "Are they real? I always used to think it was all a yarn about such things."

"I'm sure I don't know what it all means, Tammy," I answered. "I'm just as much in the dark, there, as you are. And I don't know whether they're real—that is, not as we consider things real. You don't know that I saw a queer figure down on the maindeck, several nights before you saw that thing up here."

"Didn't you see this one?" he cut in, quickly.

"Yes," I answered.

"Then, why did you pretend not to have?" he said, in a reproachful voice. "You don't know what a state you put me into, what with my being certain that I had seen it and then you being so jolly positive that there had been nothing. At one time I thought I was going clean off my dot—until the Second Mate saw that man go up the main. Then, I knew that there must be something in the thing I was certain I'd seen."

"I thought, perhaps, that if I told you I hadn't seen it, you would think you'd been mistaken," I said. "I wanted you to think it was imagination, or a dream, or something of that sort."

"And all the time, you knew about that other thing you'd seen?" he asked.

"Yes," I replied.

"It was thundering decent of you," he said. "But it wasn't any good."

He paused a moment. Then he went on:

"It's terrible about Williams. Do you think he saw something, up aloft?"

"I don't know, Tammy," I said. "It's impossible to say. It may have been only an accident." I hesitated to tell him what I really thought.

"What was he saying about his pay-day? Who was he saying it to?"

"I don't know," I said, again. "He was always cracked about taking a pay-day out of her. You know, he stayed in her, on purpose, when all the others left. He told me that he wasn't going to be done out of it, for anyone."

"What did the other lot leave for?" he asked. Then, as the idea seemed to strike him—"Jove! do you think they saw something, and got scared? It's quite possible. You know, we only joined her in 'Frisco. She had no 'prentices on the passage out. Our ship was sold; so they sent us aboard here to come home."

"They may have," I said. "Indeed, from things I've heard Williams say, I'm pretty certain, he for one, guessed or knew a jolly sight more than we've any idea of."

"And now he's dead!" said Tammy, solemnly. "We'll never be able to find out from him now."

For a few moments, he was silent. Then he went off on another track.

"Doesn't anything ever happen in the Mate's watch?"

"Yes," I answered. "There's several things happened lately, that seem pretty queer. Some of his side have been talking about them. But he's too jolly pig-headed to see anything. He just curses his chaps, and puts it all down to them."

"Still," he persisted, "things seem to happen more in our watch than in his—I mean, bigger things. Look at tonight."

"We've no proof, you know," I said.

He shook his head, doubtfully.

"I shall always funk going aloft, now."

"Nonsense!" I told him. "It may only have been an accident."

"Don't!" he said. "You know you don't think so, really."

I answered nothing, just then; for I knew very well that he was right. We were silent for a couple of moments.

Then he spoke again:

"Is the ship haunted?"

For an instant I hesitated.

"No," I said, at length. "I don't think she is. I mean, not in that way."

"What way, then?"

"Well, I've formed a bit of a theory, that seems wise one minute, and cracked the next. Of course, it's as likely to be all wrong; but it's the only thing that seems to me to fit in with all the beastly things we've had lately."

"Go on!" he said, with an impatient, nervous movement.

"Well, I've an idea that it's nothing in the ship that's likely to hurt us. I scarcely know how to put it; but, if I'm right in what I think, it's the ship herself that's the cause of everything."

"What do you mean?" he asked, in a puzzled voice. "Do you mean that the ship is haunted, after all?"

"No!" I answered. "I've just told you I didn't. Wait until I've finished what I was going to say."

"All right!" he said.

"About that thing you saw tonight," I went on. "You say it came over the lee rail, up on to the poop?"

"Yes," he answered.

"Well, the thing I saw, came up out of the sea, and went back into the sea."

"Jove!" he said; and then: "Yes, go on!"

"My idea is, that this ship is open to be boarded by those things," I explained. "What they are, of course I don't know. They look like men— in lots of ways. But—well, the Lord knows what's in the sea. Though we don't want to go imagining silly things, of course. And then, again, you know, it seems fat-headed, calling anything silly. That's how I keep going, in a sort of blessed circle. I don't know a bit whether they're flesh and blood, or whether they're what we should call ghosts or spirits."

"They can't be flesh and blood," Tammy interrupted. "Where would they live? Besides, that first one I saw, I thought I could see through it. And this last one—the Second Mate would have seen it. And they would drown—"

"Not necessarily," I said.

"Oh, but I'm sure they're not," he insisted. "It's impossible—"

"So are ghosts—when you're feeling sensible," I answered. "But I'm not saying they are flesh and blood; though, at the same time, I'm not going to say straight out they're ghosts—not yet, at any rate."

"Where do they come from?" he asked, stupidly enough.

"Out of the sea," I told him. "You saw for yourself!"

"Then why don't other vessels have them coming aboard?" he said. "How do you account for that?"

"In a way—though sometimes it seems cracky—I think I can, according to my idea," I answered.

"How?" he inquired again.

"Why, I believe that this ship is open, as I've told you—exposed, unprotected, or whatever you like to call it. I should say it's reasonable to think that all the things of the material world are barred, as it were, from the immaterial; but that in some cases the barrier may be broken down. That's what may have happened to this ship. And if it has, she may be naked to the attacks of beings belonging to some other state of existence."

"What's made her like that?" he asked, in a really awed sort of tone.

"The Lord knows!" I answered. "Perhaps something to do with magnetic stresses; but you'd not understand, and I don't, really. And, I suppose, inside of me, I don't believe it's anything of the kind, for a minute. I'm not built that way. And yet I don't know! Perhaps, there may have been some rotten thing done aboard of her. Or, again, it's a heap more likely to be something quite outside of anything I know."

"If they're immaterial then, they're spirits?" he questioned.

"I don't know," I said. "It's so hard to say what I really think, you know. I've got a queer idea, that my head-piece likes to think good; but I don't believe my tummy believes it."

"Go on!" he said.

"Well," I said. "Suppose the earth were inhabited by two kinds of life. We're one, and they're the other."

"Go on!" he said.

"Well," I said. "Don't you see, in a normal state we may not be capable of appreciating the realness of the other? But they may be just as real and material to them, as we are to us. Do you see?"

"Yes," he said. "Go on!"

"Well," I said. "The earth may be just as real to them, as to us. I mean that it may have qualities as material to them, as it has to us; but neither of us could appreciate the other's realness, or the quality of realness in the earth, which was real to the other. It's so difficult to explain. Don't you understand?"

"Yes," he said. "Go on!"

"Well, if we were in what I might call a healthy atmosphere, they would be quite beyond our power to see or feel, or anything. And the same with them; but the more we're like this, the more real and actual they could grow to us. See? That is, the more we should become able to appreciate their form of materialness. That's all. I can't make it any clearer."

"Then, after all, you really think they're ghosts, or something of that sort?" Tammy said.

"I suppose it does come to that," I answered. "I mean that, anyway, I don't think they're our ideas of flesh and blood. But, of course, it's silly to say much; and, after all, you must remember that I may be all wrong."

"I think you ought to tell the Second Mate all this," he said. "If it's really as you say, the ship ought to be put into the nearest port, and jolly well burnt."

"The Second Mate couldn't do anything," I replied. "Even if he believed it all; which we're not certain he would."

"Perhaps not," Tammy answered. "But if you could get him to believe it, he might explain the whole business to the Skipper, and then something might be done. It's not safe as it is."

"He'd only get jeered at again," I said, rather hopelessly.

"No," said Tammy. "Not after what's happened tonight."

"Perhaps not," I replied, doubtfully. And just then the Second Mate came back on to the poop, and Tammy cleared away from the wheel-box, leaving me with a worrying feeling that I ought to do something.

The Coming of the Mist and That Which It Ushered

We buried Williams at midday. Poor beggar! It had been so sudden. All day the men were awed and gloomy, and there was a lot of talk about there being a Jonah aboard. If they'd only known what Tammy and I, and perhaps the Second Mate, knew!

And then the next thing came—the mist. I cannot remember now, whether it was on the day we buried Williams that we first saw it, or the day after.

When first I noticed it, like everybody else aboard, I took it to be some form of haze, due to the heat of the sun; for it was broad daylight when the thing came.

The wind had died away to a light breeze, and I was working at the main rigging, along with Plummer, putting on seizings.

"Looks as if 'twere middlin' 'ot," he remarked.

"Yes," I said; and, for the time, took no further notice.

Presently he spoke again:

"It's gettin' quite 'azy!" and his tone showed he was surprised.

I glanced up, quickly. At first, I could see nothing. Then, I saw what he meant. The air had a wavy, strange, unnatural appearance; something like the heated air over the top of an engine's funnel, that you can often see when no smoke is coming out.

"Must be the heat," I said. "Though I don't remember ever seeing anything just like it before."

"Nor me," Plummer agreed.

It could not have been a minute later when I looked up again, and was astonished to find that the whole ship was surrounded by a thinnish haze that quite hid the horizon.

"By Jove! Plummer," I said. "How queer!"

"Yes," he said, looking round. "I never seen anythin' like it before— not in these parts."

"Heat wouldn't do that!" I said.

"N—no," he said, doubtfully.

We went on with our work again—occasionally exchanging an odd word or two. Presently, after a little time of silence, I bent forward and asked him to pass me up the spike. He stooped and picked it up from the deck, where it had tumbled. As he held it out to me, I saw the stolid expression on his face, change suddenly to a look of complete surprise. He opened his mouth.

"By gum!" he said. "It's gone."

I turned quickly, and looked. And so it had—the whole sea showing clear and bright, right away to the horizon.

I stared at Plummer, and he stared at me.

"Well, I'm blowed!" he exclaimed.

I do not think I made any reply; for I had a sudden, queer feeling that the thing was not right. And then, in a minute, I called myself an ass; but I could not really shake off the feeling. I had another good look at the sea. I had a vague idea that something was different. The sea looked brighter, somehow, and the air clearer, I thought, and I missed something; but not much, you know. And it was not until a couple of days later, that I knew that it was several vessels on the horizon, which had been quite in sight before the mist, and now were gone.

During the rest of the watch, and indeed all day, there was no further sign of anything unusual. Only, when the evening came (in the second dog-watch it was) I saw the mist rise faintly—the setting sun shining through it, dim and unreal.

I knew then, as a certainty, that it was not caused by heat.

And that was the beginning of it.

The next day, I kept a pretty close watch, during all my time on deck; but the atmosphere remained clear. Yet, I heard from one of the chaps in the Mate's watch, that it had been hazy during part of the time he was at the wheel.

"Comin' an' goin', like," he described it to me, when I questioned him about it. He thought it might be heat.

But though I knew otherwise, I did not contradict him. At that time, no one, not even Plummer, seemed to think very much of the matter. And when I mentioned it to Tammy, and asked him whether he'd noticed it, he only remarked that it must have been heat, or else the sun drawing up water. I let it stay at that; for there was nothing to be gained by suggesting that the thing had more to it.

Then, on the following day, something happened that set me wondering more than ever, and showed me how right I had been in feeling the mist to be something unnatural. It was in this way.

Five bells, in the eight to twelve morning watch, had gone. I was at the wheel. The sky was perfectly clear—not a cloud to be seen, even on the horizon. It was hot, standing at the wheel; for there was scarcely any wind, and I was feeling drowsy. The Second Mate was down on the maindeck with the men, seeing about some job he wanted done; so that I was on the poop alone.

Presently, with the heat, and the sun beating right down on to me, I grew thirsty; and, for want of something better, I pulled out a bit of plug I had on me, and bit off a chew; though, as a rule, it is not a habit of mine. After a little, naturally enough, I glanced round for the spittoon; but discovered that it was not there. Probably it had been taken forrard when the decks were washed, to give it a scrub. So, as there was no one on the poop, I left the wheel, and stepped aft to the taffrail. It was thus that I came to see something altogether unthought of—a full-rigged ship, close-hauled on the port tack, a few hundred yards on our starboard quarter. Her sails were scarcely filled by the light breeze, and flapped as she lifted to the swell of the sea. She appeared to have very little way through the water, certainly not more than a knot an hour. Away aft, hanging from the gaff-end, was a string of flags. Evidently, she was signalling to us. All this, I saw in a flash, and I just stood and stared, astonished. I was astonished because I had not seen her earlier. In that light breeze, I knew that she must have been in sight for at least a couple of hours. Yet I could think of nothing rational to satisfy my wonder. There she was—of that much, I was certain. And yet, how had she come there without my seeing her, before?

All at once, as I stood, staring, I heard the wheel behind me, spin rapidly. Instinctively, I jumped to get hold of the spokes; for I did not want the steering gear jammed. Then I turned again to have another look at the other ship; but, to my utter bewilderment, there was no sign of her—nothing but the calm ocean, spreading away to the distant horizon. I blinked my eyelids a bit, and pushed the hair off my forehead. Then, I stared again; but there was no vestige of her— nothing, you know; and absolutely nothing unusual, except a faint, tremulous quiver in the air. And the blank surface of the sea reaching everywhere to the empty horizon.

Had she foundered? I asked myself, naturally enough; and, for the moment, I really wondered. I searched round the sea for wreckage; but there was nothing, not even an odd hen-coop, or a piece of deck furniture; and so I threw away that idea, as impossible.

Then, as I stood, I got another thought, or, perhaps, an intuition and I asked myself seriously whether this disappearing ship might not be in some way connected with the other queer things. It occurred to me then, that the vessel I had seen was nothing real, and, perhaps, did not exist outside of my own brain. I considered the idea, gravely. It helped to explain the thing, and I could think of nothing else that would. Had she been real, I felt sure that others aboard us would have been bound to have seen her long before I had—I got a bit muddled there, with trying to think it out; and then, abruptly, the reality of the other ship, came back to me—every rope and sail and spar, you know. And I remembered how she had lifted to the heave of the sea, and how the sails had flapped in the light breeze. And the string of flags! She had been signalling. At that last, I found it just as impossible to believe that she had not been real.

I had reached to this point of irresolution, and was standing with my back, partly turned to the wheel. I was holding it steady with my left hand, while I looked over the sea, to try to find something to help me to understand.

All at once, as I stared, I seemed to see the ship again.

She was more on the beam now, than on the quarter; but I thought little of that, in the astonishment of seeing her once more. It was only a glimpse, I caught of her—dim and wavering, as though I looked at her through the convolutions of heated air. Then she grew indistinct, and vanished again; but I was convinced now that she was real, and had been in sight all the time, if I could have seen her. That curious, dim, wavering appearance had suggested something to me. I remembered the strange, wavy look of the air, a few days previously, just before the mist had surrounded the ship. And in my mind, I connected the two. It was nothing about the other packet that was strange. The strangeness was with us. It was something that was about (or invested) our ship that prevented me—or indeed, any one else aboard from seeing that other. It was evident that she had been able to see us, as was proved by her signalling. In an irrelevant sort of way, I wondered what the people aboard of her thought of our apparently intentional disregard of their signals.

After that, I thought of the strangeness of it all. Even at that minute, they could see us, plainly; and yet, so far as we were concerned, the whole ocean seemed empty. It appeared to me, at that time, to be the weirdest thing that could happen to us.

And then a fresh thought came to me. How long had we been like that? I puzzled for a few moments. It was now that I recollected that we had sighted several vessels on the morning of the day when the mist appeared; and since then, we had seen nothing. This, to say the least, should have struck me as queer; for some of the other packets were homeward bound along with us, and steering the same course. Consequently, with the weather being fine, and the wind next to nothing, they should have been in sight all the time. This reasoning seemed to me to show, unmistakably, some connection between the coming of the mist, and our inability to see. So that it is possible we had been in that extraordinary state of blindness for nearly three days.

In my mind, the last glimpse of that ship on the quarter, came back to me. And, I remember, a curious thought got me, that I had looked at her from out of some other dimension. For a while, you know, I really believed the mystery of the idea, and that it might be the actual truth, took me; instead of my realising just all that it might mean. It seemed so exactly to express all the half-defined thoughts that had come, since seeing that other packet on the quarter.

Suddenly, behind me, there came a rustle and rattle of the sails; and, in the same instant, I heard the Skipper saying:

"Where the devil have you got her to, Jessop?"

I whirled round to the wheel.

"I don't know—Sir," I faltered.

I had forgotten even that I was at the wheel.

"Don't know!" he shouted. "I should damned well think you don't. Starboard your helm, you fool. You'll have us all aback!"

"i, i, Sir," I answered, and hove the wheel over. I did it almost mechanically; for I was still dazed, and had not yet had time to collect my senses.

During the following half-minute, I was only conscious, in a confused sort of way, that the Old Man was ranting at me. This feeling of bewilderment passed off, and I found that I was peering blankly into the binnacle, at the compass-card; yet, until then, entirely without being aware of the fact. Now, however, I saw that the ship was coming back on to her course. Goodness knows how much she had been off!

With the realisation that I had let the ship get almost aback, there came a sudden memory of the alteration in the position of the other vessel. She had appeared last on the beam, instead of on the quarter. Now, however, as my brain began to work, I saw the cause of this apparent and, until then, inexplicable change. It was due, of course, to our having come up, until we had brought the other packet on to the beam.

It is curious how all this flashed through my mind, and held my attention—although only momentarily—in the face of the Skipper's storming. I think I had hardly realised he was still singing out at me. Anyhow, the next thing I remember, he was shaking my arm.

"What's the matter with you, man?" he was shouting. And I just stared into his face, like an ass, without saying a word. I seemed still incapable, you know, of actual, reasoning speech.

"Are you damned well off your head?" he went on shouting. "Are you a lunatic? Have you had sunstroke? Speak, you gaping idiot!"

I tried to say something; but the words would not come clearly.

"I—I—I—" I said, and stopped, stupidly. I was all right, really; but I was so bewildered with the thing I had found out; and, in a way, I seemed almost to have come back out of a distance, you know.

"You're a lunatic!" he said, again. He repeated the statement several times, as if it were the only thing that sufficiently expressed his opinion of me. Then he let go of my arm, and stepped back a couple of paces.

"I'm not a lunatic!" I said, with a sudden gasp. "I'm not a lunatic, Sir, any more than you are."

"Why the devil don't you answer my questions then?" he shouted, angrily.
"What's the matter with you? What have you been doing with the ship? Answer me now!"

"I was looking at that ship away on the starboard quarter, Sir," I blurted out. "She's been signalling—"

"What!" he cut me short with disbelief. "What ship?"

He turned, quickly, and looked over the quarter. Then he wheeled round to me again.

"There's no ship! What do you mean by trying to spin up a cuffer like that?"

"There is, Sir," I answered. "It's out there—" I pointed.

"Hold your tongue!" he said. "Don't talk rubbish to me. Do you think I'm blind?"

"I saw it, Sir," I persisted.

"Don't you talk back to me!" he snapped, with a quick burst of temper. "I won't have it!"

Then, just as suddenly, he was silent. He came a step towards me, and stared into my face. I believe the old ass thought I was a bit mad; anyway, without another word, he went to the break of the poop.

"Mr. Tulipson," he sung out.

"Yes, Sir," I heard the Second Mate reply.

"Send another man to the wheel."

"Very good, Sir," the Second answered.

A couple of minutes later, old Jaskett came up to relieve me. I gave him the course, and he repeated it.

"What's up, mate?" he asked me, as I stepped off the grating.

"Nothing much," I said, and went forrard to where the Skipper was standing on the break of the poop. I gave him the course; but the crabby old devil took no notice of me, whatever. When I got down on to the maindeck, I went up to the Second, and gave it to him. He answered me civilly enough, and then asked me what I had been doing to put the Old Man's back up.

"I told him there's a ship on the starboard quarter, signalling us," I said.

"There's no ship out there, Jessop," the Second Mate replied, looking at me with a queer, inscrutable expression.

"There is, Sir," I began. "I—"

"That will do, Jessop!" he said. "Go forrard and have a smoke. I shall want you then to give a hand with these foot-ropes. You'd better bring a serving-mallet aft with you, when you come."

I hesitated a moment, partly in anger; but more, I think, in doubt.

"i, i, Sir," I muttered at length, and went forrard.

After the Coming of the Mist

After the coming of the mist, things seemed to develop pretty quickly. In the following two or three days a good deal happened.

On the night of the day on which the Skipper had sent me away from the wheel, it was our watch on deck from eight o' clock to twelve, and my look-out from ten to twelve.

As I paced slowly to and fro across the fo'cas'le head, I was thinking about the affair of the morning. At first, my thoughts were about the Old Man. I cursed him thoroughly to myself, for being a pig-headed old fool, until it occurred to me that if I had been in his place, and come on deck to find the ship almost aback, and the fellow at the wheel staring out across the sea, instead of attending to his business, I should most certainly have kicked up a thundering row. And then, I had been an ass to tell him about the ship. I should never have done such a thing, if I had not been a bit adrift. Most likely the old chap thought I was cracked.

I ceased to bother my head about him, and fell to wondering why the Second Mate had looked at me so queerly in the morning. Did he guess more of the truth than I supposed? And if that were the case, why had he refused to listen to me?

After that, I went to puzzling about the mist. I had thought a great deal about it, during the day. One idea appealed to me, very strongly. It was that the actual, visible mist was a materialised expression of an extraordinarily subtle atmosphere, in which we were moving.

Abruptly, as I walked backwards and forwards, taking occasional glances over the sea (which was almost calm), my eye caught the glow of a light out in the darkness. I stood still, and stared. I wondered whether it was the light of a vessel. In that case we were no longer enveloped in that extraordinary atmosphere. I bent forward, and gave the thing my more immediate attention. I saw then that it was undoubtedly the green light of a vessel on our port bow. It was plain that she was bent on crossing our bows. What was more, she was dangerously near—the size and brightness of her light showed that. She would be close-hauled, while we were going free, so that, of course, it was our place to get out of her way. Instantly, I turned and, putting my hands up to my mouth, hailed the Second Mate:

"Light on the port bow, Sir."

The next moment his hail came back:

"Whereabouts?"

"He must be blind," I said to myself.

"About two points on the bow, Sir," I sung out.

Then I turned to see whether she had shifted her position at all. Yet, when I came to look, there was no light visible. I ran forrard to the bows, and leant over the rail, and stared; but there was nothing— absolutely nothing except the darkness all about us. For perhaps a few seconds I stood thus, and a suspicion swept across me, that the whole business was practically a repetition of the affair of the morning. Evidently, the impalpable something that invested the ship, had thinned for an instant, thus allowing me to see the light ahead. Now, it had closed again. Yet, whether I could see, or not, I did not doubt the fact that, there was a vessel ahead, and very close ahead, too. We might run on top of her any minute. My only hope was that, seeing we were not getting out of her way, she had put her helm up, so as to let us pass, with the intention of then crossing under our stern. I waited, pretty anxiously, watching and listening. Then, all at once, I heard steps coming along the deck, forrard, and the 'prentice, whose time-keeping it was, came up on to the fo'cas'le head.

"The Second Mate says he can't see any light Jessop," he said, coming over to where I stood. "Whereabouts is it?"

"I don't know," I answered. "I've lost sight of it myself. It was a green light, about a couple of points on the port bow. It seemed fairly close."

"Perhaps their lamp's gone out," he suggested, after peering out pretty hard into the night for a minute or so.

"Perhaps," I said.

I did not tell him that the light had been so close that, even in the darkness, we should now have been able to see the ship herself.

"You're quite sure it was a light, and not a star?" he asked, doubtfully, after another long stare.

"Oh! no," I said. "It may have been the moon, now I come to think about it."

"Don't rot," he replied. "It's easy enough to make a mistake. What shall I say to the Second Mate?"

"Tell him it's disappeared, of course!"

"Where to?" he asked.

"How the devil should I know?" I told him. "Don't ask silly questions!"

"All right, keep your rag in," he said, and went aft to report to the Second Mate.

Five minutes later, it might have been, I saw the light again. It was broad on the bow, and told me plainly enough that she had up with her helm to escape being run down. I did not wait a moment; but sung out to the Second Mate that there was a green light about four points on the port bow. By Jove! it must have been a close shave. The light did not seem to be more than about a hundred yards away. It was fortunate that we had not much way through the water.

"Now," I thought to myself, "the Second will see the thing. And perhaps Mr. Blooming 'prentice will be able to give the star its proper name."

Even as the thought came into my head, the light faded and vanished; and

I caught the Second Mate's voice.

"Whereaway?" he was singing out.

"It's gone again, Sir," I answered.

A minute later, I heard him coming along the deck.

He reached the foot of the starboard ladder.

"Where are you, Jessop?" he inquired.

"Here, Sir," I said, and went to the top of the weather ladder.

He came up slowly on to the fo'cas'le head.

"What's this you've been singing out about a light?" he asked. "Just point out exactly where it was you last saw it."

This I did, and he went over to the port rail, and stared away into the night; but without seeing anything.

"It's gone, Sir," I ventured to remind him. "Though I've seen it twice now—once, about a couple of points on the bow, and this last time, broad away on the bow; but it disappeared both times, almost at once."

"I don't understand it at all, Jessop," he said, in a puzzled voice. "Are you sure it was a ship's light?"

"Yes, Sir. A green light. It was quite close."

"I don't understand," he said again. "Run aft and ask the 'prentice to pass you down my night glasses. Be as smart as you can."

"i, i, Sir," I replied, and ran aft.

In less than a minute, I was back with his binoculars; and, with them, he stared for some time at the sea to leeward.

All at once he dropped them to his side, and faced round on me with a sudden question:

"Where's she gone to? If she's shifted her bearing as quickly as all that, she must be precious close. We should be able to see her spars and sails, or her cabin light, or her binnacle light, or something!"

"It's queer, Sir," I assented.

"Damned queer," he said. "So damned queer that I'm inclined to think you've made a mistake."

"No, Sir. I'm certain it was a light."

"Where's the ship then?" he asked.

"I can't say, Sir. That's just what's been puzzling me."

The Second said nothing in reply; but took a couple of quick turns across the fo'cas'le head—stopping at the port rail, and taking another look to leeward through his night glasses. Perhaps a minute he stood there. Then, without a word, he went down the lee ladder, and away aft along the main deck to the poop.

"He's jolly well puzzled," I thought to myself. "Or else he thinks I've been imagining things." Either way, I guessed he'd think that.

In a little, I began to wonder whether, after all, he had any idea of what might be the truth. One minute, I would feel certain he had; and the next, I was just as sure that he guessed nothing. I got one of my fits of asking myself whether it would not have been better to have told him everything. It seemed to me that he must have seen sufficient to make him inclined to listen to me. And yet, I could not by any means be certain. I might only have been making an ass of myself, in his eyes. Or set him thinking I was dotty.

I was walking about the fo'cas'le head, feeling like this, when I saw the light for the third time. It was very bright and big, and I could see it move, as I watched. This again showed me that it must be very close.

"Surely," I thought, "the Second Mate must see it now, for himself."

I did not sing out this time, right away. I thought I would let the Second see for himself that I had not been mistaken. Besides, I was not going to risk its vanishing again, the instant I had spoken. For quite half a minute, I watched it, and there was no sign of its disappearing. Every moment, I expected to hear the Second Mate's hail, showing that he had spotted it at last; but none came.

I could stand it no longer, and I ran to the rail, on the after part of the fo'cas'le head.

"Green light a little abaft the beam, Sir!" I sung out, at the top of my voice.

But I had waited too long. Even as I shouted, the light blurred and vanished.

I stamped my foot and swore. The thing was making a fool of me. Yet, I had a faint hope that those aft had seen it just before it disappeared; but this I knew was vain, directly I heard the Second's voice.

"Light be damned!" he shouted.

Then he blew his whistle, and one of the men ran aft, out of the fo'cas'le, to see what it was he wanted.

"Whose next look-out is it?" I heard him ask.

"Jaskett's, Sir."

"Then tell Jaskett to relieve Jessop at once. Do you hear?"

"Yes, Sir," said the man, and came forrard.

In a minute, Jaskett stumbled up onto the fo'cas'le head.

"What's up, mate?" he asked sleepily.

"It's that fool of a Second Mate!" I said, savagely. "I've reported a light to him three times, and, because the blind fool can't see it, he's sent you up to relieve me!"

"Where is it, mate?" he inquired.

He looked round at the dark sea.

"I don't see no light," he remarked, after a few moments.

"No," I said. "It's gone."

"Eh?" he inquired.

"It's gone!" I repeated, irritably.

He turned and regarded me silently, through the dark.

"I'd go an' 'ave a sleep, mate," he said, at length. "I've been that way meself. Ther's nothin' like a snooze w'en yer gets like that."

"What!" I said. "Like what?"

"It's all right, mate. Yer'll be all right in ther mornin'. Don't yer worry 'bout me." His tone was sympathetic.

"Hell!" was all I said, and walked down off the fo'cas'le head. I wondered whether the old fellow thought I was going silly.

"Have a sleep, by Jove!" I muttered to myself. "I wonder who'd feel like having a sleep after what I've seen and stood today!"

I felt rotten, with no one understanding what was really the matter. I seemed to be all alone, through the things I had learnt. Then the thought came to me to go aft and talk the matter over with Tammy. I knew he would be able to understand, of course; and it would be such a relief.

On the impulse, I turned and went aft, along the deck to the 'prentices' berth. As I neared the break of the poop, I looked up and saw the dark shape of the Second Mate, leaning over the rail above me.

"Who's that?" he asked.

"It's Jessop, Sir," I said.

"What do you want in this part of the ship?" he inquired.

"I'd come aft to speak to Tammy, Sir," I replied.

"You go along forrard and turn-in," he said, not altogether unkindly. "A sleep will do you more good than yarning about. You know, you're getting to fancy things too much!"

"I'm sure I'm not, Sir! I'm perfectly well. I—"

"That will do!" he interrupted, sharply. "You go and have a sleep."

I gave a short curse, under my breath, and went slowly forrard. I was getting maddened with being treated as if I were not quite sane.

"By God!" I said to myself. "Wait till the fools know what I know—just wait!"

I entered the fo'cas'le, through the port doorway, and went across to my chest, and sat down. I felt angry and tired, and miserable.

Quoin and Plummer were sitting close by, playing cards, and smoking. Stubbins lay in his bunk, watching them, and also smoking. As I sat down, he put his head forward over the bunk-board, and regarded me in a curious, meditative way.

"What's hup with ther Second hoffücer?" he asked, after a short stare.

I looked at him, and the other two men looked up at me. I felt I should go off with a bang, if I did not say something, and I let out pretty stiffly, telling them the whole business. Yet, I had seen enough to know that it was no good trying to explain things; so I just told them the plain, bold facts, and left explanations as much alone as possible.

"Three times, you say?" said Stubbins when I had finished.

"Yes," I assented.

"An' ther Old Man sent yer from ther wheel this mornin', 'cause yer 'appened ter see a ship 'e couldn't," Plummer added in a reflective tone.

"Yes," I said, again.

I thought I saw him look at Quoin, significantly; but Stubbins, I noticed, looked only at me.

"I reckon ther Second thinks you're a bit hoff colour," he remarked, after a short pause.

"The Second Mate's a fool!" I said, with some bitterness. "A confounded fool!"

"I hain't so sure about that," he replied. "It's bound ter seem queer ter him. I don't understand it myself—"

He lapsed into silence, and smoked.

"I carn't understand 'ow it is ther Second Mate didn't 'appen to spot it," Quoin said, in a puzzled voice.

It seemed to me that Plummer nudged him to be quiet. It looked as if Plummer shared the Second Mate's opinion, and the idea made me savage. But Stubbins's next remark drew my attention.

"I don't hunderstand it," he said, again; speaking with deliberation. "All ther same, ther Second should have savvied enough not to have slung you hoff ther look-hout."

He nodded his head, slowly, keeping his gaze fixed on my face.

"How do you mean?" I asked, puzzled; yet with a vague sense that the man understood more, perhaps, than I had hitherto thought.

"I mean what's ther Second so blessed cocksure about?"

He took a draw at his pipe, removed it, and leant forward somewhat, over his bunk-board.

"Didn't he say nothin' ter you, after you came hoff ther look-hout?" he asked.

"Yes," I replied; "he spotted me going aft. He told me I was getting to imagining things too much. He said I'd better come forrard and get a sleep."

"An' what did you say?"

"Nothing. I came forrard."

"Why didn't you bloomin' well harsk him if he weren't doin' ther imaginin' trick when he sent us chasin' hup ther main, hafter that bogyman of his?"

"I never thought of it," I told him.

"Well, yer ought ter have."

He paused, and sat up in his bunk, and asked for a match.

As I passed him my box, Quoin looked up from his game.

"It might 'ave been a stowaway, yer know. Yer carn't say as it's ever been proved as it wasn't."

Stubbins passed the box back to me, and went on without noticing Quoin's remark:

"Told you to go an' have a snooze, did he? I don't hunderstand what he's bluffin' at."

"How do you mean, bluffing?" I asked.

He nodded his head, sagely.

"It's my hidea he knows you saw that light, just as bloomin' well as I do."

Plummer looked up from his game, at this speech; but said nothing.

"Then you don't doubt that I really saw it?" I asked, with a certain surprise.

"Not me," he remarked, with assurance. "You hain't likely ter make that kind of mistake three times runnin'."

"No," I said. "I know I saw the light, right enough; but"—I hesitated a moment—"it's blessed queer."

"It is blessed queer!" he agreed. "It's damned queer! An' there's a lot of other damn queer things happenin' aboard this packet lately."

He was silent for a few seconds. Then he spoke suddenly:

"It's not nat'ral, I'm damned sure of that much."

He took a couple of draws at his pipe, and in the momentary silence, I caught Jaskett's voice, above us. He was hailing the poop.

"Red light on the starboard quarter, Sir," I heard him sing out.

"There you are," I said with a jerk of my head. "That's about where that packet I spotted, ought to be by now. She couldn't cross our bows, so she up helm, and let us pass, and now she's hauled up again and gone under our stern."

I got up from the chest, and went to the door, the other three following. As we stepped out on deck, I heard the Second Mate shouting out, away aft, to know the whereabouts of the light.

"By Jove! Stubbins," I said. "I believe the blessed thing's gone again."

We ran to the starboard side, in a body, and looked over; but there was no sign of a light in the darkness astern.

"I carn't say as I see any light," said Quoin.

Plummer said nothing.

I looked up at the fo'cas'le head. There, I could faintly distinguish the outlines of Jaskett. He was standing by the starboard rail, with his hands up, shading his eyes, evidently staring towards the place where he had last seen the light.

"Where's she got to, Jaskett?" I called out.

"I can't say, mate," he answered. "It's the most 'ellishly funny thing I've ever comed across. She were there as plain as me 'att one minnit, an' ther next she were gone—clean gone."

I turned to Plummer.

"What do you think about it, now?" I asked him.

"Well," he said. "I'll admit I thought at first 'twere somethin' an' nothin'. I thought yer was mistaken; but it seems yer did see somethin'."

Away aft, we heard the sound of steps, along the deck.

"Ther Second's comin' forrard for a hexplanation, Jaskett," Stubbins sung out. "You'd better go down an' change yer breeks."

The Second Mate passed us, and went up the starboard ladder.

"What's up now, Jaskett?" he said quickly. "Where is this light? Neither the 'prentice nor I can see it!"

"Ther damn thing's clean gone, Sir," Jaskett replied.

"Gone!" the Second Mate said. "Gone! What do you mean?"

"She were there one minnit, Sir, as plain as me 'att, an' ther next, she'd gone."

"That's a damn silly yarn to tell me!" the Second replied. "You don't expect me to believe it, do you?"

"It's Gospel trewth any'ow, Sir," Jaskett answered. "An' Jessop seen it just ther same."

He seemed to have added that last part as an afterthought. Evidently, the old beggar had changed his opinion as to my need for sleep.

"You're an old fool, Jaskett," the Second said, sharply. "And that idiot Jessop has been putting things into your silly old head."

He paused, an instant. Then he continued:

"What the devil's the matter with you all, that you've taken to this sort of game? You know very well that you saw no light! I sent Jessop off the look-out, and then you must go and start the same game."

"We 'aven't—" Jaskett started to say; but the Second silenced him.

"Stow it!" he said, and turned and went down the ladder, passing us quickly, without a word.

"Doesn't look to me, Stubbins," I said, "as though the Second did believe we've seen the light."

"I hain't so sure," he answered. "He's a puzzler."

The rest of the watch passed away quietly; and at eight bells I made haste to turn-in, for I was tremendously tired.

When we were called again for the four to eight watch on deck, I learnt that one of the men in the Mate's watch had seen a light, soon after we had gone below, and had reported it, only for it to disappear immediately. This, I found, had happened twice, and the Mate had got so wild (being under the impression that the man was playing the fool) that he had nearly came to blows with him—finally ordering him off the look-out, and sending another man up in his place. If this last man saw the light, he took good care not to let the Mate know; so that the matter had ended there.

And then, on the following night, before we had ceased to talk about the matter of the vanishing lights, something else occurred that temporarily drove from my mind all memory of the mist, and the extraordinary, blind atmosphere it had seemed to usher.

The Man Who Cried for Help

It was, as I have said, on the following night that something further happened. And it brought home pretty vividly to me, if not to any of the others, the sense of a personal danger aboard.

We had gone below for the eight to twelve watch, and my last impression of the weather at eight o'clock, was that the wind was freshening. There had been a great bank of cloud rising astern, which had looked as if it were going to breeze up still more.

At a quarter to twelve, when we were called for our twelve to four watch on deck, I could tell at once, by the sound, that there was a fresh breeze blowing; at the same time, I heard the voices of the men on the other watch, singing out as they hauled on the ropes. I caught the rattle of canvas in the wind, and guessed that they were taking the royals off her. I looked at my watch, which I always kept hanging in my bunk. It showed the time to be just after the quarter; so that, with luck, we should escape having to go up to the sails.

I dressed quickly, and then went to the door to look at the weather. I found that the wind had shifted from the starboard quarter, to right aft; and, by the look of the sky, there seemed to be a promise of more, before long.

Up aloft, I could make out faintly the fore and mizzen royals flapping in the wind. The main had been left for a while longer. In the fore riggings, Jacobs, the Ordinary Seaman in the Mate's watch, was following another of the men aloft to the sail. The Mate's two 'prentices were already up at the mizzen. Down on deck, the rest of the men were busy clearing up the ropes.

I went back to my bunk, and looked at my watch—the time was only a few minutes off eight bells; so I got my oilskins ready, for it looked like rain outside. As I was doing this, Jock went to the door for a look.

"What's it doin', Jock?" Tom asked, getting out of his bunk, hurriedly.

"I'm thinkin' maybe it's goin' to blow a wee, and ye'll be needin' yer' oilskins," Jock answered.

When eight bells went, and we mustered aft for roll-call, there was a considerable delay, owing to the Mate refusing to call the roll until Tom (who as usual, had only turned out of his bunk at the last minute) came aft to answer his name. When, at last, he did come, the Second and the Mate joined in giving him a good dressing down for a lazy sojer; so that several minutes passed before we were on our way forrard again. This was a small enough matter in itself, and yet really terrible in its consequence to one of our number; for, just as we reached the fore rigging, there was a shout aloft, loud above the noise of the wind, and the next moment, something crashed down into our midst, with a great, slogging thud—something bulky and weighty, that struck full upon Jock, so that he went down with a loud, horrible, ringing "ugg," and never said a word. From the whole crowd of us there went up a yell of fear, and then, with one accord, there was a run for the lighted fo'cas'le. I am not ashamed to say that I ran with the rest. A blind, unreasoning fright had seized me, and I did not stop to think.

Once in the fo'cas'le and the light, there was a reaction. We all stood and looked blankly at one another for a few moments. Then someone asked a question, and there was a general murmur of denial. We all felt ashamed, and someone reached up and unhooked the lantern on the port side. I did the same with the starboard one; and there was a quick movement towards the doors. As we streamed out on deck, I caught the sound of the Mates' voices. They had evidently come down from off the poop to find out what had happened; but it was too dark to see their whereabouts.

"Where the hell have you all got to?" I heard the Mate shout.

The next instant, they must have seen the light from our lanterns; for I heard their footsteps, coming along the deck at a run. They came the starboard side, and just abaft the fore rigging, one of them stumbled and fell over something. It was the First Mate who had tripped. I knew this by the cursing that came directly afterwards. He picked himself up, and, apparently without stopping to see what manner of thing it was that he had fallen over, made a rush to the pin-rail. The Second Mate ran into the circle of light thrown by our lanterns, and stopped, dead— eyeing us doubtfully. I am not surprised at this, now, nor at the behaviour of the Mate, the following instant; but at that time, I must say I could not conceive what had come to them, particularly the First Mate. He came out at us from the darkness with a rush and a roar like a bull and brandishing a belaying-pin. I had failed to take into account the scene which his eyes must have shown him:—the whole crowd of men in the fo'cas'le—both watches—pouring out on to the deck in utter confusion, and greatly excited, with a couple of fellows at their head, carrying lanterns. And before this, there had been the cry aloft and the crash down on deck, followed by the shouts of the frightened crew, and the sounds of many feet running. He may well have taken the cry for a signal, and our actions for something not far short of mutiny. Indeed, his words told us that this was his very thought.

"I'll knock the face off the first man that comes a step further aft!" he shouted, shaking the pin in my face. "I'll show yer who's master here! What the hell do yer mean by this? Get forrard into yer kennel!"

There was a low growl from the men at the last remark, and the old bully stepped back a couple of paces.

"Hold on, you fellows!" I sung out. "Shut up a minute."

"Mr. Tulipson!" I called out to the Second, who had not been able to get a word in edgeways, "I don't know what the devil's the matter with the First Mate; but he'll not find it pay to talk to a crowd like ours, in that sort of fashion, or there'll be ructions aboard."

"Come! come! Jessop! This won't do! I can't have you talking like that about the Mate!" he said, sharply. "Let me know what's to-do, and then go forrard again, the lot of you."

"We'd have told you at first, Sir," I said, "only the Mate wouldn't give any of us a chance to speak. There's been an awful accident, Sir. Something's fallen from aloft, right on to Jock—"

I stopped suddenly; for there was a loud crying aloft.

"Help! help! help!" someone was shouting, and then it rose from a shout into a scream.

"My God! Sir!" I shouted. "That's one of the men up at the fore royal!"

"Listen!" ordered the Second Mate. "Listen!" Even as he spoke, it came again—broken and, as it were, in gasps.

"Help!... Oh!... God!... Oh!... Help! H-e-l-p!"

Abruptly, Stubbins's voice struck in.

"Hup with us, lads! By God! hup with us!" and he made a spring into the fore rigging. I shoved the handle of the lantern between my teeth, and followed. Plummer was coming; but the Second Mate pulled him back.

"That's sufficient," he said. "I'm going," and he came up after me.

We went over the foretop, racing like fiends. The light from the lantern prevented me from seeing to any distance in the darkness; but, at the crosstrees, Stubbins, who was some ratlines ahead, shouted out all at once, and in gasps:

"They're fightin' ... like ... hell!"

"What?" called the Second Mate, breathlessly.

Apparently, Stubbins did not hear him; for he made no reply. We cleared the crosstrees, and climbed into the t'gallant rigging. The wind was fairly fresh up there, and overhead, there sounded the flap, flap of sailcloth flying in the wind; but since we had left the deck, there had been no other sound from above.

Now, abruptly, there came again a wild crying from the darkness over us. A strange, wild medley it was of screams for help, mixed up with violent, breathless curses.

Beneath the royal yard, Stubbins halted, and looked down to me.

"Hurry hup ... with ther ... lantern ... Jessop!" he shouted, catching his breath between the words. "There'll be ... murder done ... hin a minute!"

I reached him, and held the light up for him to catch. He stooped, and took it from me. Then, holding it above his head, he went a few ratlines higher. In this manner, he reached to a level with the royal yard. From my position, a little below him, the lantern seemed but to throw a few straggling, flickering rays along the spar; yet they showed me something. My first glance had been to wind'ard, and I had seen at once, that there was nothing on the weather yard arm. From there my gaze went to leeward. Indistinctly, I saw something upon the yard, that clung, struggling. Stubbins bent towards it with the light; thus I saw it more clearly. It was Jacobs, the Ordinary Seaman. He had his right arm tightly round the yard; with the other, he appeared to be fending himself from something on the other side of him, and further out upon the yard. At times, moans and gasps came from him, and sometimes curses. Once, as he appeared to be dragged partly from his hold, he screamed like a woman. His whole attitude suggested stubborn despair. I can scarcely tell you how this extraordinary sight affected me. I seemed to stare at it without realising that the affair was a real happening.

During the few seconds which I had spent staring and breathless, Stubbins had climbed round the after side of the mast, and now I began again to follow him.

From his position below me, the Second had not been able to see the thing that was occurring on the yard, and he sung out to me to know what was happening.

"It's Jacobs, Sir," I called back. "He seems to be fighting with someone to looard of him. I can't see very plainly yet."

Stubbins had got round on to the lee foot-rope, and now he held the lantern up, peering, and I made my way quickly alongside of him. The Second Mate followed; but instead of getting down on to the foot-rope, he got on the yard, and stood there holding on to the tie. He sung out for one of us to pass him up the lantern, which I did, Stubbins handing it to me. The Second held it out at arm's length, so that it lit up the lee part of the yard. The light showed through the darkness, as far as to where Jacobs struggled so weirdly. Beyond him, nothing was distinct.

There had been a moment's delay while we were passing the lantern up to the Second Mate. Now, however, Stubbins and I moved out slowly along the foot-rope. We went slowly; but we did well to go at all, with any show of boldness; for the whole business was so abominably uncanny. It seems impossible to convey truly to you, the strange scene on the royal yard. You may be able to picture it yourselves. The Second Mate standing upon the spar, holding the lantern; his body swaying with each roll of the ship, and his head craned forward as he peered along the yard. On our left, Jacobs, mad, fighting, cursing, praying, gasping; and outside of him, shadows and the night.

The Second Mate spoke, abruptly.

"Hold on a moment!" he said. Then:

"Jacobs!" he shouted. "Jacobs, do you hear me?"

There was no reply, only the continual gasping and cursing.

"Go on," the Second Mate said to us. "But be careful. Keep a tight hold!"

He held the lantern higher and we went out cautiously.

Stubbins reached the Ordinary, and put his hand on his shoulder, with a soothing gesture.

"Steady hon now, Jacobs," he said. "Steady hon."

At his touch, as though by magic, the young fellow calmed down, and Stubbins—reaching round him—grasped the jackstay on the other side.

"Get a hold of him your side, Jessop," he sung out. "I'll get this side."

This, I did, and Stubbins climbed round him.

"There hain't no one here," Stubbins called to me; but his voice expressed no surprise.

"What!" sung out the Second Mate. "No one there! Where's Svensen, then?"

I did not catch Stubbins's reply; for suddenly, it seemed to me that I saw something shadowy at the extreme end of the yard, out by the lift. I stared. It rose up, on the yard, and I saw that it was the figure of a man. It grasped at the lift, and commenced to swarm up, quickly. It passed diagonally above Stubbins's head, and reached down a vague hand and arm.

"Look out! Stubbins!" I shouted. "Look out!"

"What's up now?" he called, in a startled voice. At the same instant, his cap went whirling away to leeward.

"Damn the wind!" he burst out.

Then all at once, Jacobs, who had only been giving an occasional moan, commenced to shriek and struggle.

"Hold fast onto him!" Stubbins yelled. "He'll be throwin' himself off the yard."

I put my left arm round the Ordinary's body—getting hold of the jackstay on the other side. Then I looked up. Above us, I seemed to see something dark and indistinct, that moved rapidly up the lift.

"Keep tight hold of him, while I get a gasket," I heard the Second Mate sing out.

A moment later there was a crash, and the light disappeared.

"Damn and set fire to the sail!" shouted the Second Mate.

I twisted round, somewhat, and looked in his direction. I could dimly make him out on the yard. He had evidently been in the act of getting down on to the foot-rope, when the lantern was smashed. From him, my gaze jumped to the lee rigging. It seemed that I made out some shadowy thing stealing down through the darkness; but I could not be sure; and then, in a breath, it had gone.

"Anything wrong, Sir?" I called out.

"Yes," he answered. "I've dropped the lantern. The blessed sail knocked it out of my hand!"

"We'll be all right, Sir," I replied. "I think we can manage without it. Jacobs seems to be quieter now."

"Well, be careful as you come in," he warned us.

"Come on, Jacobs," I said. "Come on; we'll go down on deck."

"Go along, young feller," Stubbins put in. "You're right now. We'll take care of you." And we started to guide him along the yard.

He went willingly enough, though without saying a word. He seemed like a child. Once or twice he shivered; but said nothing.

We got him in to the lee rigging. Then, one going beside him, and the other keeping below, we made our way slowly down on deck. We went very slowly—so slowly, in fact, that the Second Mate—who had stayed a minute to shove the gasket round the lee side of the sail—was almost as soon down.

"Take Jacobs forrard to his bunk," he said, and went away aft to where a crowd of the men, one with a lantern, stood round the door of an empty berth under the break of the poop on the starboard side.

We hurried forrard to the fo'cas'le. There we found all in darkness.

"They're haft with Jock, and Svenson!" Stubbins had hesitated an instant before saying the name.

"Yes," I replied. "That's what it must have been, right enough."

"I kind of knew it all ther time," he said.

I stepped in through the doorway, and struck a match. Stubbins followed, guiding Jacobs before him, and, together, we got him into his bunk. We covered him up with his blankets, for he was pretty shivery. Then we came out. During the whole time, he had not spoken a word.

As we went aft, Stubbins remarked that he thought the business must have made him a bit dotty.

"It's driven him clean barmy," he went on. "He don't hunderstand a word that's said ter him."

"He may be different in the morning," I answered.

As we neared the poop, and the crowd of waiting men, he spoke again:

"They've put 'em hinter ther Second's hempty berth."

"Yes," I said. "Poor beggars."

We reached the other men, and they opened out, and allowed us to get near the door. Several of them asked in low tones, whether Jacobs was all right, and I told them, "Yes"; not saying anything then about his condition.

I got close up to the doorway, and looked into the berth. The lamp was lit, and I could see, plainly. There were two bunks in the place, and a man had been laid in each. The Skipper was there, leaning up against a bulkshead. He looked worried; but was silent—seeming to be mooding in his own thoughts. The Second Mate was busy with a couple of flags, which he was spreading over the bodies. The First Mate was talking, evidently telling him something; but his tone was so low that I caught his words only with difficulty. It struck me that he seemed pretty subdued. I got parts of his sentences in patches, as it were.

"...broken," I heard him say. "And the Dutchman...."

"I've seen him," the Second Mate said, shortly.

"Two, straight off the reel," said the Mate "...three in...."

The Second made no reply.

"Of course, yer know ... accident." The First Mate went on.

"Is it!" the Second said, in a queer voice.

I saw the Mate glance at him, in a doubtful sort of way; but the Second was covering poor old Jock's dead face, and did not appear to notice his look.

"It—it—" the mate said, and stopped.

After a moment's hesitation, he said something further, that I could not catch; but there seemed a lot of funk in his voice.

The Second Mate appeared not to have heard him; at any rate, he made no reply; but bent, and straightened out a corner of the flag over the rigid figure in the lower bunk. There was a certain niceness in his action which made me warm towards him.

"He's white!" I thought to myself.

Out loud, I said:

"We've put Jacobs into his bunk, Sir."

The Mate jumped; then whizzed round, and stared at me as though I had been a ghost. The Second Mate turned also; but before he could speak, the Skipper took a step towards me.

"Is he all right?" he asked.

"Well, Sir," I said. "He's a bit queer; but I think it's possible he may be better, after a sleep."

"I hope so, too," he replied, and stepped out on deck. He went towards the starboard poop ladder, walking slowly. The Second went and stood by the lamp, and the Mate, after a quick glance at him, came out and followed the Skipper up on to the poop. It occurred to me then, like a flash, that the man had stumbled upon a portion of the truth. This accident coming so soon after that other! It was evident that, in his mind, he had connected them. I recollected the fragments of his remarks to the Second Mate. Then, those many minor happenings that had cropped up at different times, and at which he had sneered. I wondered whether he would begin to comprehend their significance—their beastly, sinister significance.

"Ah! Mr. Bully-Mate," I thought to myself. "You're in for a bad time if you've begun to understand."

Abruptly, my thoughts jumped to the vague future before us.

"God help us!" I muttered.

The Second Mate, after a look round, turned down the wick of the lamp, and came out, closing the door after him.

"Now, you men," he said to the Mate's watch, "get forrard; we can't do anything more. You'd better go and get some sleep."

"i, i, Sir," they said, in a chorus.

Then, as we all turned to go forrard, he asked if anyone had relieved the look-out.

"No, sir," answered Quoin.

"Is it yours?" the Second asked.

"Yes, Sir," he replied.

"Hurry up and relieve him then," the Second said.

"i, i, Sir," the man answered, and went forrard with the rest of us.

As we went, I asked Plummer who was at the wheel.

"Tom," he said.

As he spoke, several spots of rain fell, and I glanced up at the sky. It had become thickly clouded.

"Looks as if it were going to breeze up," I said.

"Yes," he replied. "We'll be shortenin' 'er down 'fore long."

"May be an all-hands job," I remarked.

"Yes," he answered again. "'Twon't be no use their turnin' in, if it is."

The man who was carrying the lantern, went into the fo'cas'le, and we followed.

"Where's ther one, belongin' to our side?" Plummer asked.

"Got smashed hupstairs," answered Stubbins.

"'ow were that?" Plummer inquired.

Stubbins hesitated.

"The Second Mate dropped it," I replied. "The sail hit it, or something."

The men in the other watch seemed to have no immediate intention of turning-in; but sat in their bunks, and around on the chests. There was a general lighting of pipes, in the midst of which there came a sudden moan from one of the bunks in the forepart of the fo'cas'le—a part that was always a bit gloomy, and was more so now, on account of our having only one lamp.

"Wot's that?" asked one of the men belonging to the other side.

"S—sh!" said Stubbins. "It's him."

"'oo?" inquired Plummer. "Jacobs?"

"Yes," I replied. "Poor devil!"

"Wot were 'appenin' w'en yer got hup ther'?" asked the man on the other side, indicating with a jerk of his head, the fore royal.

Before I could reply, Stubbins jumped up from his sea-chest.

"Ther Second Mate's whistlin'!" he said. "Come hon," and he ran out on deck.

Plummer, Jaskett and I followed quickly. Outside, it had started to rain pretty heavily. As we went, the Second Mate's voice came to us through the darkness.

"Stand by the main royal clewlines and buntlines," I heard him shout, and the next instant came the hollow thutter of the sail as he started to lower away.

In a few minutes we had it hauled up.

"Up and furl it, a couple of you," he sung out.

I went towards the starboard rigging; then I hesitated. No one else had moved.

The Second Mate came among us.

"Come on now, lads," he said. "Make a move. It's got to be done."

"I'll go," I said. "If someone else will come."

Still, no one stirred, and no one answered.

Tammy came across to me.

"I'll come," he volunteered, in a nervous voice.

"No, by God, no!" said the Second Mate, abruptly.

He jumped into the main rigging himself. "Come along, Jessop!" he shouted.

I followed him; but I was astonished. I had fully expected him to get on to the other fellows' tracks like a ton of bricks. It had not occurred to me that he was making allowances. I was simply puzzled then; but afterwards it dawned upon me.

No sooner had I followed the Second Mate, than, straightway, Stubbins, Plummer, and Jaskett came up after us at a run.

About half-way to the maintop, the Second Mate stopped, and looked down.

"Who's that coming up below you, Jessop?" he asked.

Before I could, speak, Stubbins answered:

"It's me, Sir, an' Plummer an' Jaskett."

"Who the devil told you to come now? Go straight down, the lot of you!"

"We're comin' hup ter keep you company, Sir," was his reply.

At that, I was confident of a burst of temper from the Second; and yet, for the second time within a couple of minutes I was wrong. Instead of cursing Stubbins, he, after a moment's pause, went on up the rigging, without another word, and the rest of us followed. We reached the royal, and made short work of it; indeed, there were sufficient of us to have eaten it. When we had finished, I noticed that the Second Mate remained on the yard until we were all in the rigging. Evidently, he had determined to take a full share of any risk there might be; but I took care to keep pretty close to him; so as to be on hand if anything happened; yet we reached the deck again, without anything having occurred. I have said, without anything having occurred; but I am not really correct in this; for, as the Second Mate came down over the crosstrees, he gave a short, abrupt cry.

"Anything wrong, Sir?" I asked.

"No—o!" he said. "Nothing! I banged my knee."

And yet now, I believe he was lying. For, that same watch, I was to hear men giving just such cries; but, God knows, they had reason enough.

Hands That Plucked

Directly we reached the deck, the Second Mate gave the order:

"Mizzen t'gallant clewlines and buntlines," and led the way up on to the poop. He went and stood by the haulyards, ready to lower away. As I walked across to the starboard clewline, I saw that the Old Man was on deck, and as I took hold of the rope, I heard him sing out to the Second Mate.

"Call all hands to shorten sail, Mr. Tulipson."

"Very good, Sir," the Second Mate replied. Then he raised his voice:

"Go forrard, you, Jessop, and call all hands to shorten sail. You'd better give them a call in the bosun's place, as you go."

"i, i, Sir," I sung out, and hurried off.

As I went, I heard him tell Tammy to go down and call the Mate.

Reaching the fo'cas'le, I put my head in through the starboard doorway, and found some of the men beginning to turn-in.

"It's all hands on deck, shorten sail," I sung out.

I stepped inside.

"Just wot I said," grumbled one of the men.

"They don't damn well think we're goin' aloft to-night, after what's happened?" asked another.

"We've been up to the main royal," I answered. "The Second Mate went with us."

"Wot?" said the first man. "Ther Second Mate hisself?"

"Yes," I replied. "The whole blooming watch went up."

"An' wot 'appened?" he asked.

"Nothing," I said. "Nothing at all. We just made a mouthful apiece of it, and came down again."

"All the same," remarked the second man, "I don't fancy goin' upstairs, after what's happened."

"Well," I replied. "It's not a matter of fancy. We've got to get the sail off her, or there'll be a mess. One of the 'prentices told me the glass is falling."

"Come erlong, boys. We've got ter du it," said one of the older men, rising from a chest, at this point. "What's it duin' outside, mate?"

"Raining," I said. "You'll want your oilskins."

I hesitated a moment before going on deck again. From the bunk forrard among the shadows, I had seemed to hear a faint moan.

"Poor beggar!" I thought to myself.

Then the old chap who had last spoken, broke in upon my attention.

"It's awl right, mate!" he said, rather testily. "Yer needn't wait. We'll be out in er minit."

"That's all right. I wasn't thinking about you lot," I replied, and walked forrard to Jacobs's bunk. Some time before, he had rigged up a pair of curtains, cut out of an old sack, to keep off the draught. These, some one had drawn, so that I had to pull them aside to see him. He was lying on his back, breathing in a queer, jerky fashion. I could not see his face, plainly; but it seemed rather pale, in the half-light.

"Jacobs," I said. "Jacobs, how do you feel now?" but he made no sign to show that he had heard me. And so, after a few moments, I drew the curtains to again, and left him.

"What like does 'e seem?" asked one of the fellows, as I went towards the door.

"Bad," I said. "Damn bad! I think the Steward ought to be told to come and have a look at him. I'll mention it to the Second when I get a chance."

I stepped out on deck, and ran aft again to give them a hand with the sail. We got it hauled up, and then went forrard to the fore t'gallant. And, a minute later, the other watch were out, and, with the Mate, were busy at the main.

By the time the main was ready for making fast, we had the fore hauled up, so that now all three t'gallants were in the ropes, and ready for stowing. Then came the order:

"Up aloft and furl!"

"Up with you, lads," the Second Mate said. "Don't let's have any hanging back this time."

Away aft by the main, the men in the Mate's watch seemed to be standing in a clump by the mast; but it was too dark to see clearly. I heard the Mate start to curse; then there came a growl, and he shut up.

"Be handy, men! be handy!" the Second Mate sung out.

At that, Stubbins jumped into the rigging.

"Come hon!" he shouted. "We'll have ther bloomin' sail fast, an' down hon deck again before they're started."

Plummer followed; then Jaskett, I, and Quoin who had been called down off the look-out to give a hand.

"That's the style, lads!" the Second sung out, encouragingly. Then he ran aft to the Mate's crowd. I heard him and the Mate talking to the men, and presently, when we were going over the foretop, I made out that they were beginning to get into the rigging.

I found out, afterwards, that as soon as the Second Mate had seen them off the deck, he went up to the mizzen t'gallant, along with the four 'prentices.

On our part, we made our way slowly aloft, keeping one hand for ourselves and the other for the ship, as you can fancy. In this manner we had gone as far as the crosstrees, at least, Stubbins, who was first, had; when, all at once, he gave out just another such cry as had the Second Mate a little earlier, only that in his case he followed it by turning round and blasting Plummer.

"You might have blarsted well sent me flyin' down hon deck," he shouted.

"If you bl—dy well think it's a joke, try it hon some one else—"

"It wasn't me!" interrupted Plummer. "I 'aven't touched yer. 'oo the 'ell are yer swearin' at?"

"At you—!" I heard him reply; but what more he may have said, was lost in a loud shout from Plummer.

"What's up, Plummer?" I sung out. "For God's sake, you two, don't get fighting, up aloft!"

But a loud, frightened curse was all the answer he gave. Then straightway, he began to shout at the top of his voice, and in the lulls of his noise, I caught the voice of Stubbins, cursing savagely.

"They'll come down with a run!" I shouted, helplessly. "They'll come down as sure as nuts."

I caught Jaskett by the boot.

"What are they doing? What are they doing?" I sung out. "Can't you see?" I shook his leg as I spoke. But at my touch, the old idiot—as I thought him at the moment—began to shout in a frightened voice:

"Oh! oh! help! hel—!"

"Shut up!" I bellowed. "Shut up, you old fool. If you won't do anything, let me get past you."

Yet he only cried out the more. And then, abruptly, I caught the sound of a frightened clamour of men's voices, away down somewhere about the maintop—curses, cries of fear, even shrieks, and above it all, someone shouting to go down on deck:

"Get down! get down! down! down! Blarst—" The rest was drowned in a fresh outburst of hoarse crying in the night.

I tried to get past old Jaskett; but he was clinging to the rigging, sprawled on to it, is the best way to describe his attitude, so much of it as I could see in the darkness. Up above him, Stubbins and Plummer still shouted and cursed, and the shrouds quivered and shook, as though the two were fighting desperately.

Stubbins seemed to be shouting something definite; but whatever it was, I could not catch.

At my helplessness, I grew angry, and shook and prodded Jaskett, to make him move.

"Damn you, Jaskett!" I roared. "Damn you for a funky old fool! Let me get past! Let me get past, will you!"

But, instead of letting me pass, I found that he was beginning to make his way down. At that, I caught him by the slack of his trousers, near the stern, with my right hand, and with the other, I got hold of the after shroud somewhere above his left hip; by these means, I fairly hoisted myself up on to the old fellow's back. Then, with my right, I could reach to the forrard shroud, over his right shoulder, and having got a grip, I shifted my left to a level with it; at the same moment, I was able to get my foot on to the splice of a ratline and so give myself a further lift. Then I paused an instant, and glanced up.

"Stubbins! Stubbins!" I shouted. "Plummer! Plummer!"

And even as I called, Plummer's foot—reaching down through the gloom— alighted full on my upturned face. I let go from the rigging with my right hand, and struck furiously at his leg, cursing him for his clumsiness. He lifted his foot, and in the same instant a sentence from Stubbins floated down to me, with a strange distinctness:

"For God's sake tell 'em to get down hon deck!" he was shouting.

Even as the words came to me, something in the darkness gripped my waist. I made a desperate clutch at the rigging with my disengaged right hand, and it was well for me that I secured the hold so quickly, for the same instant, I was wrenched at with a brutal ferocity that appalled me. I said nothing, but lashed out into the night with my left foot. It is queer, but I cannot say with certainty that I struck anything; I was too downright desperate with funk, to be sure; and yet it seemed to me that my foot encountered something soft, that gave under the blow. It may have been nothing more than an imagined sensation; yet I am inclined to think otherwise; for, instantly, the hold about my waist was released; and I commenced to scramble down, clutching the shrouds pretty desperately.

I have only a very uncertain remembrance of that which followed. Whether I slid over Jaskett, or whether he gave way to me, I cannot tell. I know only that I reached the deck, in a blind whirl of fear and excitement, and the next thing I remember, I was among a crowd of shouting, half-mad sailor-men.

THE SEARCH FOR STUBBINS

In a confused way, I was conscious that the Skipper and the Mates were down among us, trying to get us into some state of calmness. Eventually they succeeded, and we were told to go aft to the Saloon door, which we did in a body. Here, the Skipper himself served out a large tot of rum to each of us. Then, at his orders, the Second Mate called the roll.

He called over the Mate's watch first, and everyone answered. Then he came to ours, and he must have been much agitated; for the first name he sung out was Jock's.

Among us there came a moment of dead silence, and I noticed the wail and moan of the wind aloft, and the flap, flap of the three unfurled t'gallan's'ls.

The Second Mate called the next name, hurriedly:

"Jaskett," he sung out.

"Sir," Jaskett answered.

"Quoin."

"Yes, Sir."

"Jessop."

"Sir," I replied.

"Stubbins."

There was no answer.

"Stubbins," again called the Second Mate.

Again there was no reply.

"Is Stubbins here?—anyone!" The Second's voice sounded sharp and anxious.

There was a moment's pause. Then one of the men spoke:

"He's not here, Sir."

"Who saw him last?" the Second asked.

Plummer stepped forward into the light that streamed through the Saloon doorway. He had on neither coat nor cap, and his shirt seemed to be hanging about him in tatters.

"It were me, Sir," he said.

The Old Man, who was standing next to the Second Mate, took a pace towards him, and stopped and stared; but it was the Second who spoke.

"Where?" he asked.

"'e were just above me, in ther crosstrees, when, when—" the man broke off short.

"Yes! yes!" the Second Mate replied. Then he turned to the Skipper.

"Someone will have to go up, Sir, and see—" He hesitated.

"But—" said the Old Man, and stopped.

The Second Mate cut in.

"I shall go up, for one, Sir," he said, quietly.

Then he turned back to the crowd of us.

"Tammy," he sung out. "Get a couple of lamps out of the lamp-locker."

"i, i, Sir," Tammy replied, and ran off.

"Now," said the Second Mate, addressing us. "I want a couple of men to jump aloft along with me and take a look for Stubbins."

Not a man replied. I would have liked to step out and offer; but the memory of that horrible clutch was with me, and for the life of me, I could not summon up the courage.

"Come! come, men!" he said. "We can't leave him up there. We shall take lanterns. Who'll come now?"

I walked out to the front. I was in a horrible funk; but, for very shame, I could not stand back any longer.

"I'll come with you, Sir," I said, not very loud, and feeling fairly twisted up with nervousness.

"That's more the tune, Jessop!" he replied, in a tone that made me glad I had stood out.

At this point, Tammy came up, with the lights. He brought them to the Second, who took one, and told him to give the other to me. The Second Mate held his light above his head, and looked round at the hesitating men.

"Now, men!" he sung out. "You're not going to let Jessop and me go up alone. Come along, another one or two of you! Don't act like a damned lot of cowards!"

Quoin stood out, and spoke for the crowd.

"I dunno as we're actin' like cowyards, Sir; but just look at 'im," and he pointed at Plummer, who still stood full in the light from the Saloon doorway.

"What sort of a Thing is it 'as done that, Sir?" he went on. "An' then yer arsks us ter go up agen! It aren't likely as we're in a 'urry."

The Second Mate looked at Plummer, and surely, as I have before mentioned, the poor beggar was in a state; his ripped-up shirt was fairly flapping in the breeze that came through the doorway.

The Second looked; yet he said nothing. It was as though the realisation of Plummer's condition had left him without a word more to say. It was Plummer himself who finally broke the silence.

"I'll come with yer, Sir," he said. "Only yer ought ter 'ave more light than them two lanterns. 'Twon't be no use, unless we 'as plenty er light."

The man had grit; and I was astonished at his offering to go, after what he must have gone through. Yet, I was to have even a greater astonishment; for, abruptly, The Skipper—who all this time had scarcely spoken—stepped forward a pace, and put his hand on the Second Mate's shoulder.

"I'll come with you, Mr. Tulipson," he said.

The Second Mate twisted his head round, and stared at him a moment, in astonishment. Then he opened his mouth.

"No, Sir; I don't think—" he began.

"That's sufficient, Mr. Tulipson," the Old Man interrupted. "I've made up my mind."

He turned to the First Mate, who had stood by without a word.

"Mr. Grainge," he said. "Take a couple of the 'prentices down with you, and pass out a box of blue-lights and some flare-ups."

The Mate answered something, and hurried away into the Saloon, with the two 'prentices in his watch. Then the Old Man spoke to the men.

"Now, men!" he began. "This is no time for dilly-dallying. The Second Mate and I will go aloft, and I want about half a dozen of you to come along with us, and carry lights. Plummer and Jessop here, have volunteered. I want four or five more of you. Step out now, some of you!"

There was no hesitation whatever, now; and the first man to come forward was Quoin. After him followed three of the Mate's crowd, and then old Jaskett.

"That will do; that will do," said the Old Man.

He turned to the Second Mate.

"Has Mr. Grainge come with those lights yet?" he asked, with a certain irritability.

"Here, Sir," said the First Mate's voice, behind him in the Saloon doorway. He had the box of blue-lights in his hands, and behind him, came the two boys carrying the flares.

The Skipper took the box from him, with a quick gesture, and opened it.

"Now, one of you men, come here," he ordered.

One of the men in the Mate's watch ran to him.

He took several of the lights from the box, and handed them to the man.

"See here," he said. "When we go aloft, you get into the foretop, and keep one of these going all the time, do you hear?"

"Yes, Sir," replied the man.

"You know how to strike them?" the Skipper asked, abruptly.

"Yes, Sir," he answered.

The Skipper sung out to the Second Mate:

"Where's that boy of yours—Tammy, Mr. Tulipson?"

"Here, Sir," said Tammy, answering for himself.

The Old Man took another light from the box.

"Listen to me, boy!" he said. "Take this, and stand-by on the forrard deck house. When we go aloft, you must give us a light until the man gets his going in the top. You understand?"

"Yes, Sir," answered Tammy, and took the light.

"One minute!" said the Old Man, and stooped and took a second light from the box. "Your first light may go out before we're ready. You'd better have another, in case it does."

Tammy took the second light, and moved away.

"Those flares all ready for lighting there, Mr. Grainge?" the Captain asked.

"All ready, Sir," replied the Mate.

The Old Man pushed one of the blue-lights into his coat pocket, and stood upright.

"Very well," he said. "Give each of the men one apiece. And just see that they all have matches."

He spoke to the men particularly:

"As soon as we are ready, the other two men in the Mate's watch will get up into the cranelines, and keep their flares going there. Take your paraffin tins with you. When we reach the upper topsail, Quoin and Jaskett will get out on the yard-arms, and show their flares there. Be careful to keep your lights away from the sails. Plummer and Jessop will come up with the Second Mate and myself. Does every man clearly understand?"

"Yes, Sir," said the men in a chorus.

A sudden idea seemed to occur to the Skipper, and he turned, and went through the doorway into the Saloon. In about a minute, he came back, and handed something to the Second Mate, that shone in the light from the lanterns. I saw that it was a revolver, and he held another in his other hand, and this I saw him put into his side pocket.

The Second Mate held the pistol a moment, looking a bit doubtful.

"I don't think, Sir—" he began. But the Skipper cut him short.

"You don't know!" he said. "Put it in your pocket."

Then he turned to the First Mate.

"You will take charge of the deck, Mr. Grainge, while we're aloft," he said.

"i, i, Sir," the Mate answered and sung out to one of his 'prentices to take the blue-light box back into the cabin.

The Old Man turned and led the way forrard. As we went, the light from the two lanterns shone upon the decks, showing the litter of the t'gallant gear. The ropes were foul of one another in a regular "bunch o' buffers[1]." This had been caused, I suppose, by the crowd trampling over them in their excitement, when they reached the deck. And then, suddenly, as though the sight had waked me up to a more vivid comprehension, you know, it came to me new and fresh, how damned strange was the whole business... I got a little touch of despair, and asked myself what was going to be the end of all these beastly happenings. You can understand?

[Footnote 1: Modified from the original.]

Abruptly, I heard the Skipper shouting, away forward. He was singing out to Tammy to get up on to the house with his blue-light. We reached the fore rigging, and, the same instant, the strange, ghastly flare of Tammy's blue-light burst out into the night causing every rope, sail, and spar to jump out weirdly.

I saw now that the Second Mate was already in the starboard rigging, with his lantern. He was shouting to Tammy to keep the drip from his light clear of the staysail, which was stowed upon the house. Then, from somewhere on the port side, I heard the Skipper shout to us to hurry.

"Smartly now, you men," he was saying. "Smartly now."

The man who had been told to take up a station in the fore-top, was just behind the Second Mate. Plummer was a couple of ratlines lower.

I caught the Old Man's voice again.

"Where's Jessop with that other lantern?" I heard him shout.

"Here, Sir," I sung out.

"Bring it over this side," he ordered. "You don't want the two lanterns on one side."

I ran round the fore side of the house. Then I saw him. He was in the rigging, and making his way smartly aloft. One of the Mate's watch and Quoin were with him. This, I saw as I came round the house. Then I made a jump, gripped the sheerpole, and swung myself up on to the rail. And then, all at once, Tammy's blue-light went out, and there came, what seemed by contrast, pitchy darkness. I stood where I was—one foot on the rail and my knee upon the sheerpole. The light from my lantern seemed no more than a sickly yellow glow against the gloom, and higher, some forty or fifty feet, and a few ratlines below the futtock rigging on the starboard side, there was another glow of yellowness in the night. Apart from these, all was blackness. And then from above—high above—there wailed down through the darkness a weird, sobbing cry. What it was, I do not know; but it sounded horrible.

The Skipper's voice came down, jerkily.

"Smartly with that light, boy!" he shouted. And the blue glare blazed out again, almost before he had finished speaking.

I stared up at the Skipper. He was standing where I had seen him before the light went out, and so were the two men. As I looked, he commenced to climb again. I glanced across to starboard. Jaskett, and the other man in the Mate's watch, were about midway between the deck of the house and the foretop. Their faces showed extraordinary pale in the dead glare of the blue-light. Higher, I saw the Second Mate in the futtock rigging, holding his light up over the edge of the top. Then he went further, and disappeared. The man with the blue-lights followed, and also vanished from view. On the port side, and more directly above me, the Skipper's feet were just stepping out of the futtock shrouds. At that I made haste to follow.

Then, suddenly, when I was close under the top, there came from above me the sharp flare of a blue-light, and almost in the same instant, Tammy's went out.

I glanced down at the decks. They were filled with flickering, grotesque shadows cast by the dripping light above. A group of the men stood by the port galley door—their faces upturned and pale and unreal under the gleam of the light.

Then I was in the futtock rigging, and a moment afterwards, standing in the top, beside the Old Man. He was shouting to the men who had gone out on the craneline. It seemed that the man on the port side was bungling; but at last—nearly a minute after the other man had lit his flare—he got going. In that time, the man in the top had lit his second blue-light, and we were ready to get into the topmast rigging. First, however, the Skipper leant over the afterside of the top, and sung out to the First Mate to send a man up on to the fo'cas'le head with a flare. The Mate replied, and then we started again, the Old Man leading.

Fortunately, the rain had ceased, and there seemed to be no increase in the wind; indeed, if anything, there appeared to be rather less; yet what there was drove the flames of the flare-ups out into occasional, twisting serpents of fire at least a yard long.

About half-way up the topmast rigging, the Second Mate sung out to the Skipper, to know whether Plummer should light his flare; but the Old Man said he had better wait until we reached the crosstrees, as then he could get out away from the gear to where there would be less danger of setting fire to anything.

We neared the crosstrees, and the Old Man stopped and sung out to me to pass him the lantern by Quoin. A few ratlines more, and both he and the Second Mate stopped almost simultaneously, holding their lanterns as high as possible, and peered up into the darkness.

"See any signs of him, Mr. Tulipson?" the Old Man asked.

"No, Sir," replied the Second. "Not a sign."

He raised his voice.

"Stubbins," he sung out. "Stubbins, are you there?"

We listened; but nothing came to us beyond the blowing moan of the wind, and the flap, flap of the bellying t'gallant above.

The Second Mate climbed over the crosstrees, and Plummer followed. The man got out by the royal backstay, and lit his flare. By its light we could see, plainly; but there was no vestige of Stubbins, so far as the light went.

"Get out on to the yard-arms with those flares, you two men," shouted the Skipper. "Be smart now! Keep them away from the sail!"

The men got on to the foot-ropes—Quoin on the port, and Jaskett on the starboard side. By the light from Plummer's flare, I could see them clearly, as they lay out upon the yard. It occurred to me that they went gingerly—which is no surprising thing. And then, as they drew near to the yard-arms, they passed beyond the brilliance of the light; so that I could not see them clearly. A few seconds passed, and then the light from Quoin's flare streamed out upon the wind; yet nearly a minute went by, and there was no sign of Jaskett's.

Then out from the semi-darkness at the starboard yard-arm, there came a curse from Jaskett, followed almost immediately by a noise of something vibrating.

"What's up?" shouted the Second Mate. "What's up, Jaskett?"

"It's ther foot-rope, Sir-r-r!" he drew out the last word into a sort of gasp.

The Second Mate bent quickly, with the lantern. I craned round the after side of the top-mast, and looked.

"What is the matter, Mr. Tulipson?" I heard the Old Man singing out.

Out on the yard-arm, Jaskett began to shout for help, and then, all at once, in the light from the Second Mate's lantern, I saw that the starboard foot-rope on the upper topsail yard was being violently shaken—savagely shaken, is perhaps a better word. And then, almost in the same instant, the Second Mate shifted the lantern from his right to his left hand. He put the right into his pocket and brought out his gun with a jerk. He extended his hand and arm, as though pointing at something a little below the yard. Then a quick flash spat out across the shadows, followed immediately by a sharp, ringing crack. In the same moment, I saw that the foot-rope ceased to shake.

"Light your flare! Light your flare, Jaskett!" the Second shouted. "Be smart now!"

Out at the yard-arm there came a splutter of a match, and then, straightaway, a great spurt of fire as the flare took light.

"That's better, Jaskett. You're all right now!" the Second Mate called out to him.

"What was it, Mr. Tulipson?" I heard the Skipper ask.

I looked up, and saw that he had sprung across to where the Second Mate was standing. The Second Mate explained to him; but he did not speak loud enough for me to catch what he said.

I had been struck by Jaskett's attitude, when the light of his flare had first revealed him. He had been crouched with his right knee cocked over the yard, and his left leg down between it and the foot-rope, while his elbows had been crooked over the yard for support, as he was lighting the flare. Now, however, he had slid both feet back on to the foot-rope, and was lying on his belly, over the yard, with the flare held a little below the head of the sail. It was thus, with the light being on the foreside of the sail, that I saw a small hole a little below the foot-rope, through which a ray of the light shone. It was undoubtedly the hole which the bullet from the Second Mate's revolver had made in the sail.

Then I heard the Old Man shouting to Jaskett.

"Be careful with that flare there!" he sung out. "You'll be having that sail scorched!"

He left the Second Mate, and came back on to the port side of the mast.

To my right, Plummer's flares seemed to be dwindling. I glanced up at his face through the smoke. He was paying no attention to it; instead, he was staring up above his head.

"Shove some paraffin on to it, Plummer," I called to him. "It'll be out in a minute."

He looked down quickly to the light, and did as I suggested. Then he held it out at arm's length, and peered up again into the darkness.

"See anything?" asked the Old Man, suddenly observing his attitude.

Plummer glanced at him, with a start.

"It's ther r'yal, Sir," he explained. "It's all adrift."

"What!" said the Old Man.

He was standing a few ratlines up the t'gallant rigging, and he bent his body outwards to get a better look.

"Mr. Tulipson!" he shouted. "Do you know that the royal's all adrift?"

"No, Sir," answered the Second Mate. "If it is, it's more of this devilish work!"

"It's adrift right enough," said the Skipper, and he and the Second went a few ratlines higher, keeping level with one another.

I had now got above the crosstrees, and was just at the Old Man's heels. Suddenly, he shouted out:

"There he is!—Stubbins! Stubbins!"

"Where, Sir?" asked the Second, eagerly. "I can't see him!"

"There! there!" replied the Skipper, pointing.

I leant out from the rigging, and looked up along his back, in the direction his finger indicated. At first, I could see nothing; then, slowly, you know, there grew upon my sight a dim figure crouching upon the bunt of the royal, and partly hidden by the mast. I stared, and gradually it came to me that there was a couple of them, and further out upon the yard, a hump that might have been anything, and was only visible indistinctly amid the flutter of the canvas.

"Stubbins!" the Skipper sung out. "Stubbins, come down out of that! Do you hear me?"

But no one came, and there was no answer.

"There's two—" I began; but he was shouting again:

"Come down out of that! Do you damned well hear me?"

Still there was no reply.

"I'm hanged if I can see him at all, Sir!" the Second Mate called out from his side of the mast.

"Can't see him!" said the Old Man, now thoroughly angry. "I'll soon let you see him!"

He bent down to me with the lantern.

"Catch hold, Jessop," he said, which I did.

Then he pulled the blue light from his pocket, and as he was doing so, I saw the Second peek round the back side of the mast at him. Evidently, in the uncertain light, he must have mistaken the Skipper's action; for, all at once, he shouted out in a frightened voice:

"Don't shoot, Sir! For God's sake, don't shoot!"

"Shoot be damned!" exclaimed the Old Man. "Watch!"

He pulled off the cap of the light.

"There's two of them, Sir," I called again to him.

"What!" he said in a loud voice, and at the same instant he rubbed the end of the light across the cap, and it burst into fire.

He held it up so that it lit the royal yard like day, and straightway, a couple of shapes dropped silently from the royal on to the t'gallant yard. At the same moment, the humped Something, midway out upon the yard, rose up. It ran in to the mast, and I lost sight of it.

"God!" I heard the Skipper gasp, and he fumbled in his side pocket.

I saw the two figures which had dropped on to the t'gallant, run swiftly along the yard—one to the starboard and the other to the port yard-arms.

On the other side of the mast, the Second Mate's pistol cracked out twice, sharply. Then, from over my head the Skipper fired twice, and then again; but with what effect, I could not tell. Abruptly, as he fired his last shot, I was aware of an indistinct Something, gliding down the starboard royal backstay. It was descending full upon Plummer, who, all unconscious of the thing, was staring towards the t'gallant yard.

"Look out above you, Plummer!" I almost shrieked.

"What? where?" he called, and grabbed at the stay, and waved his flare, excitedly.

Down on the upper topsail yard, Quoin's and Jaskett's voices rose simultaneously, and in the identical instant, their flares went out. Then Plummer shouted, and his light went utterly. There were left only the two lanterns, and the blue-light held by the Skipper, and that, a few seconds afterwards, finished and died out.

The Skipper and the Second Mate were shouting to the men upon the yard, and I heard them answer, in shaky voices. Out on the crosstrees, I could see, by the light from my lantern, that Plummer was holding in a dazed fashion to the backstay.

"Are you all right, Plummer?" I called.

"Yes," he said, after a little pause; and then he swore.

"Come in off that yard, you men!" the Skipper was singing out. "Come in! come in!"

Down on deck, I heard someone calling; but could not distinguish the words. Above me, pistol in hand, the Skipper was glancing about, uneasily.

"Hold up that light, Jessop," he said. "I can't see!"

Below us, the men got off the yard, into the rigging.

"Down on deck with you!" ordered the Old Man.

"As smartly as you can!"

"Come in off there, Plummer!" sung out the Second Mate. "Get down with the others!"

"Down with you, Jessop!" said the Skipper, speaking rapidly. "Down with you!"

I got over the crosstrees, and he followed. On the other side, the Second Mate was level with us. He had passed his lantern to Plummer, and I caught the glint of his revolver in his right hand. In this fashion, we reached the top. The man who had been stationed there with the blue-lights, had gone. Afterwards, I found that he went down on deck as soon as they were finished. There was no sign of the man with the flare on the starboard craneline. He also, I learnt later, had slid down one of the backstays on to the deck, only a very short while before we reached the top. He swore that a great black shadow of a man had come suddenly upon him from aloft. When I heard that, I remembered the thing I had seen descending upon Plummer. Yet the man who had gone out upon the port craneline—the one who had bungled with the lighting of his flare—was still where we had left him; though his light was burning now but dimly.

"Come in out of that, you!" the Old Man sung out "Smartly now, and get down on deck!"

"i, i, Sir," the man replied, and started to make his way in.

The Skipper waited until he had got into the main rigging, and then he told me to get down out of the top. He was in the act of following, when, all at once, there rose a loud outcry on deck, and then came the sound of a man screaming.

"Get out of my way, Jessop!" the Skipper roared, and swung himself down alongside of me.

I heard the Second Mate shout something from the starboard rigging. Then we were all racing down as hard as we could go. I had caught a momentary glimpse of a man running from the doorway on the port side of the fo'cas'le. In less than half a minute we were upon the deck, and among a crowd of the men who were grouped round something. Yet, strangely enough, they were not looking at the thing among them; but away aft at something in the darkness.

"It's on the rail!" cried several voices.

"Overboard!" called somebody, in an excited voice. "It's jumped over the side!"

"Ther' wer'n't nothin'!" said a man in the crowd.

"Silence!" shouted the Old Man. "Where's the Mate? What's happened?"

"Here, Sir," called the First Mate, shakily, from near the centre of the group. "It's Jacobs, Sir. He—he—"

"What!" said the Skipper. "What!"

"He—he's—he's—dead I think!" said the First Mate, in jerks.

"Let me see," said the Old Man, in a quieter tone.

The men had stood to one side to give him room, and he knelt beside the man upon the deck.

"Pass the lantern here, Jessop," he said.

I stood by him, and held the light. The man was lying face downwards on the deck. Under the light from the lantern, the Skipper turned him over and looked at him.

"Yes," he said, after a short examination. "He's dead."

He stood up and regarded the body a moment, in silence. Then he turned to the Second Mate, who had been standing by, during the last couple of minutes.

"Three!" he said, in a grim undertone.

The Second Mate nodded, and cleared his voice.

He seemed on the point of saying something; then he turned and looked at
Jacobs, and said nothing.

"Three," repeated the Old Man. "Since eight bells!"

He stooped and looked again at Jacobs.

"Poor devil! poor devil!" he muttered.

The Second Mate grunted some of the huskiness out of his throat, and spoke.

"Where must we take him?" he asked, quietly. "The two bunks are full."

"You'll have to put him down on the deck by the lower bunk," replied the
Skipper.

As they carried him away, I heard the Old Man make a sound that was almost a groan. The rest of the men had gone forrard, and I do not think he realised that I was standing by him

"My God! O, my God!" he muttered, and began to walk slowly aft.

He had cause enough for groaning. There were three dead, and Stubbins had gone utterly and completely. We never saw him again.

THE COUNCIL

A few minutes later, the Second Mate came forrard again. I was still standing near the rigging, holding the lantern, in an aimless sort of way.

"That you, Plummer?" he asked.

"No, Sir," I said. "It's Jessop."

"Where's Plummer, then?" he inquired.

"I don't know, Sir," I answered. "I expect he's gone forrard. Shall I go and tell him you want him?"

"No, there's no need," he said. "Tie your lamp up in the rigging—on the sheerpole there. Then go and get his, and shove it up on the starboard side. After that you'd better go aft and give the two 'prentices a hand in the lamp locker."

"i, i, Sir," I replied, and proceeded to do as he directed. After I had got the light from Plummer, and lashed it up to the starboard sherpole, I hurried aft. I found Tammy and the other 'prentice in our watch, busy in the locker, lighting lamps.

"What are we doing?" I asked.

"The Old Man's given orders to lash all the spare lamps we can find, in the rigging, so as to have the decks light," said Tammy. "And a damned good job too!"

He handed me a couple of the lamps, and took two himself.

"Come on," he said, and stepped out on deck. "We'll fix these in the main rigging, and then I want to talk to you."

"What about the mizzen?" I inquired.

"Oh," he replied. "He" (meaning the other 'prentice) "will see to that. Anyway, it'll be daylight directly."

We shoved the lamps up on the sherpoles—two on each side. Then he came across to me.

"Look here, Jessop!" he said, without any hesitation. "You'll have to jolly well tell the Skipper and the Second Mate all you know about all this."

"How do you mean?" I asked.

"Why, that it's something about the ship herself that's the cause of what's happened," he replied. "If you'd only explained to the Second Mate when I told you to, this might never have been!"

"But I don't know," I said. "I may be all wrong. It's only an idea of mine. I've no proofs—"

"Proofs!" he cut in with. "Proofs! what about tonight? We've had all the proofs ever I want!"

I hesitated before answering him.

"So have I, for that matter," I said, at length. "What I mean is, I've nothing that the Skipper and the Second Mate would consider as proofs. They'd never listen seriously to me."

"They'd listen fast enough," he replied. "After what's happened this watch, they'd listen to anything. Anyway, it's jolly well your duty to tell them!"

"What could they do, anyway?" I said, despondently. "As things are going, we'll all be dead before another week is over, at this rate."

"You tell them," he answered. "That's what you've got to do. If you can only get them to realise that you're right, they'll be glad to put into the nearest port, and send us all ashore."

I shook my head.

"Well, anyway, they'll have to do something," he replied, in answer to my gesture. "We can't go round the Horn, with the number of men we've lost. We haven't enough to handle her, if it comes on to blow."

"You've forgotten, Tammy," I said. "Even if I could get the Old Man to believe I'd got at the truth of the matter, he couldn't do anything. Don't you see, if I'm right, we couldn't even see the land, if we made it. We're like blind men...."

"What on earth do you mean?" he interrupted. "How do you make out we're like blind men? Of course we could see the land—"

"Wait a minute! wait a minute!" I said. "You don't understand. Didn't I tell you?"

"Tell what?" he asked.

"About the ship I spotted," I said. "I thought you knew!"

"No," he said. "When?"

"Why," I replied. "You know when the Old Man sent me away from the wheel?"

"Yes," he answered. "You mean in the morning watch, day before yesterday?"

"Yes," I said. "Well, don't you know what was the matter?"

"No," he replied. "That is, I heard you were snoozing at the wheel, and the Old Man came up and caught you."

"That's all a darned silly yarn!" I said. And then I told him the whole truth of the affair. After I had done that, I explained my idea about it, to him.

"Now you see what I mean?" I asked.

"You mean that this strange atmosphere—or whatever it is—we're in, would not allow us to see another ship?" he asked, a bit awestruck.

"Yes," I said. "But the point I wanted you to see, is that if we can't see another vessel, even when she's quite close, then, in the same way, we shouldn't be able to see land. To all intents and purposes we're blind. Just you think of it! We're out in the middle of the briny, doing a sort of eternal blind man's hop. The Old Man couldn't put into port, even if he wanted to. He'd run us bang on shore, without our ever seeing it."

"What are we going to do, then?" he asked, in a despairing sort of way. "Do you mean to say we can't do anything? Surely something can be done! It's terrible!"

For perhaps a minute, we walked up and down, in the light from the different lanterns. Then he spoke again.

"We might be run down, then," he said, "and never even see the other vessel?"

"It's possible," I replied. "Though, from what I saw, it's evident that we're quite visible; so that it would be easy for them to see us, and steer clear of us, even though we couldn't see them."

"And we might run into something, and never see it?" he asked me, following up the train of thought.

"Yes," I said. "Only there's nothing to stop the other ship from getting out of our way."

"But if it wasn't a vessel?" he persisted. "It might be an iceberg, or a rock, or even a derelict."

"In that case," I said, putting it a bit flippantly, naturally, "we'd probably damage it."

He made no answer to this and for a few moments, we were quiet.

Then he spoke abruptly, as though the idea had come suddenly to him.

"Those lights the other night!" he said. "Were they a ship's lights?"

"Yes," I replied. "Why?"

"Why," he answered. "Don't you see, if they were really lights, we could see them?"

"Well, I should think I ought to know that," I replied. "You seem to forget that the Second Mate slung me off the look-out for daring to do that very thing."

"I don't mean that," he said. "Don't you see that if we could see them at all, it showed that the atmosphere-thing wasn't round us then?"

"Not necessarily," I answered. "It may have been nothing more than a rift in it; though, of course, I may be all wrong. But, anyway, the fact that the lights disappeared almost as soon as they were seen, shows that it was very much round the ship."

That made him feel a bit the way I did, and when next he spoke, his tone had lost its hopefulness.

"Then you think it'll be no use telling the Second Mate and the Skipper anything?" he asked.

"I don't know," I replied. "I've been thinking about it, and it can't do any harm. I've a very good mind to."

"I should," he said. "You needn't be afraid of anybody laughing at you, now. It might do some good. You've seen more than anyone else."

He stopped in his walk, and looked round.

"Wait a minute," he said, and ran aft a few steps. I saw him look up at the break of the poop; then he came back.

"Come along now," he said. "The Old Man's up on the poop, talking to the
Second Mate. You'll never get a better chance."

Still I hesitated; but he caught me by the sleeve, and almost dragged me to the lee ladder.

"All right," I said, when I got there. "All right, I'll come. Only I'm hanged if I know what to say when I get there."

"Just tell them you want to speak to them," he said. "They'll ask what you want, and then you spit out all you know. They'll find it interesting enough."

"You'd better come too," I suggested. "You'll be able to back me up in lots of things."

"I'll come, fast enough," he replied. "You go up."

I went up the ladder, and walked across to where the Skipper and the Second Mate stood talking earnestly, by the rail. Tammy kept behind. As I came near to them, I caught two or three words; though I attached no meaning then to them. They were: "...send for him." Then the two of them turned and looked at me, and the Second Mate asked what I wanted.

"I want to speak to you and the Old M—Captain, Sir," I answered.

"What is it, Jessop?" the Skipper inquired.

"I scarcely know how to put it, Sir," I said. "It's—it's about these— these things."

"What things? Speak out, man," he said.

"Well, Sir," I blurted out. "There's some dreadful thing or things come aboard this ship, since we left port."

I saw him give one quick glance at the Second Mate, and the Second looked back.

Then the Skipper replied.

"How do you mean, come aboard?" he asked.

"Out of the sea, Sir," I said. "I've seen them. So's Tammy, here."

"Ah!" he exclaimed, and it seemed to me, from his face, that he was understanding something better. "Out of the Sea!"

Again he looked at the Second Mate; but the Second was staring at me.

"Yes Sir," I said. "It's the ship. She's not safe! I've watched. I think I understand a bit; but there's a lot I don't."

I stopped. The Skipper had turned to the Second Mate. The Second nodded, gravely. Then I heard him mutter, in a low voice, and the Old Man replied; after which he turned to me again.

"Look here, Jessop," he said. "I'm going to talk straight to you. You strike me as being a cut above the ordinary shellback, and I think you've sense enough to hold your tongue."

"I've got my mate's ticket, Sir," I said, simply.

Behind me, I heard Tammy give a little start. He had not known about it until then.

The Skipper nodded.

"So much the better," he answered. "I may have to speak to you about that, later on."

He paused, and the Second Mate said something to him, in an undertone.

"Yes," he said, as though in reply to what the Second had been saying. Then he spoke to me again.

"You've seen things come out of the sea, you say?" he questioned. "Now just tell me all you can remember, from the very beginning."

I set to, and told him everything in detail, commencing with the strange figure that had stepped aboard out of the sea, and continuing my yarn, up to the things that had happened in that very watch.

I stuck well to solid facts; and now and then he and the Second Mate would look at one another, and nod. At the end, he turned to me with an abrupt gesture.

"You still hold, then, that you saw a ship the other morning, when I sent you from the wheel?" he asked.

"Yes, Sir," I said. "I most certainly do."

"But you knew there wasn't any!" he said.

"Yes, Sir," I replied, in an apologetic tone. "There was; and, if you will let me, I believe that I can explain it a bit."

"Well," he said. "Go on."

Now that I knew he was willing to listen to me in a serious manner all my funk of telling him had gone, and I went ahead and told him my ideas about the mist, and the thing it seemed to have ushered, you know. I finished up, by telling him how Tammy had worried me to come and tell what I knew.

"He thought then, Sir," I went on, "that you might wish to put into the nearest port; but I told him that I didn't think you could, even if you wanted to."

"How's that?" he asked, profoundly interested.

"Well, Sir," I replied. "If we're unable to see other vessels, we shouldn't be able to see the land. You'd be piling the ship up, without ever seeing where you were putting her."

This view of the matter, affected the Old Man in an extraordinary manner; as it did, I believe, the Second Mate. And neither spoke for a moment. Then the Skipper burst out.

"By Gad! Jessop," he said. "If you're right, the Lord have mercy on us."

He thought for a couple of seconds. Then he spoke again, and I could see that he was pretty well twisted up:

"My God!... if you're right!"

The Second Mate spoke.

"The men mustn't know, Sir," he warned him. "It'd be a mess if they did!"

"Yes," said the Old Man.

He spoke to me.

"Remember that, Jessop," he said. "Whatever you do, don't go yarning about this, forrard."

"No, Sir," I replied.

"And you too, boy," said the Skipper. "Keep your tongue between your teeth. We're in a bad enough mess, without your making it worse. Do you hear?"

"Yes, Sir," answered Tammy.

The Old Man turned to me again.

"These things, or creatures that you say come out of the sea," he said. "You've never seen them, except after nightfall?" he asked.

"No, Sir," I replied. "Never."

He turned to the Second Mate.

"So far as I can make out, Mr. Tulipson," he remarked, "the danger seems to be only at night."

"It's always been at night, Sir," the Second answered.

The Old Man nodded.

"Have you anything to propose, Mr. Tulipson?" he asked.

"Well, Sir," replied the Second Mate. "I think you ought to have her snugged down every night, before dark!"

He spoke with considerable emphasis. Then he glanced aloft, and jerked his head in the direction of the unfurled t'gallants.

"It's a damned good thing, Sir," he said, "that it didn't come on to blow any harder."

The Old Man nodded again.

"Yes," he remarked. "We shall have to do it; but God knows when we'll get home!"

"Better late than not at all," I heard the Second mutter, under his breath.

Out loud, he said:

"And the lights, Sir?"

"Yes," said the Old Man. "I will have lamps in the rigging every night, after dark."

"Very good, Sir," assented the Second. Then he turned to us.

"It's getting daylight, Jessop," he remarked, with a glance at the sky. "You'd better take Tammy with you, and shove those lamps back again into the locker."

"i, i, Sir," I said, and went down off the poop with Tammy.

The Shadow in the Sea

When eight bells went, at four o'clock, and the other watch came on deck to relieve us, it had been broad daylight for some time. Before we went below, the Second Mate had the three t'gallants set; and now that it was light, we were pretty curious to have a look aloft, especially up the fore; and Tom, who had been up to overhaul the gear, was questioned a lot, when he came down, as to whether there were any signs of anything queer up there. But he told us there was nothing unusual to be seen.

At eight o'clock, when we came on deck for the eight to twelve watch, I saw the Sailmaker coming forrard along the deck, from the Second Mate's old berth. He had his rule in his hand, and I knew he had been measuring the poor beggars in there, for their burial outfit. From breakfast time until near noon, he worked, shaping out three canvas wrappers from some old sailcloth. Then, with the aid of the Second Mate and one of the hands, he brought out the three dead chaps on to the after hatch, and there sewed them up, with a few lumps of holy stone at their feet. He was just finishing when eight bells went, and I heard the Old Man tell the Second Mate to call all hands aft for the burial. This was done, and one of the gangways unshipped.

We had no decent grating big enough, so they had to get off one of the hatches, and use it instead. The wind had died away during the morning, and the sea was almost a calm—the ship lifting ever so slightly to an occasional glassy heave. The only sounds that struck on the ear were the soft, slow rustle and occasional shiver of the sails, and the continuous and monotonous creak, creak of the spars and gear at the gentle movements of the vessel. And it was in this solemn half-quietness that the Skipper read the burial service.

They had put the Dutchman first upon the hatch (I could tell him by his stumpiness), and when at last the Old Man gave the signal, the Second Mate tilted his end, and he slid off, and down into the dark.

"Poor old Dutchie," I heard one of the men say, and I fancy we all felt a bit like that.

Then they lifted Jacobs on to the hatch, and when he had gone, Jock. When Jock was lifted, a sort of sudden shiver ran through the crowd. He had been a favourite in a quiet way, and I know I felt, all at once, just a bit queer. I was standing by the rail, upon the after bollard, and Tammy was next to me; while Plummer stood a little behind. As the Second Mate tilted the hatch for the last time, a little, hoarse chorus broke from the men:

"S'long, Jock! So long, Jock!"

And then, at the sudden plunge, they rushed to the side to see the last of him as he went downwards. Even the Second Mate was not able to resist this universal feeling, and he, too, peered over. From where I had been standing, I had been able to see the body take the water, and now, for a brief couple of seconds, I saw the white of the canvas, blurred by the blue of the water, dwindle and dwindle in the extreme depth. Abruptly, as I stared, it disappeared—too abruptly, it seemed to me.

"Gone!" I heard several voices say, and then our watch began to go slowly forrard, while one or two of the other, started to replace the hatch.

Tammy pointed, and nudged me.

"See, Jessop," he said. "What is it?"

"What?" I asked.

"That queer shadow," he replied. "Look!"

And then I saw what he meant. It was something big and shadowy, that appeared to be growing clearer. It occupied the exact place—so it seemed to me—in which Jock had disappeared.

"Look at it!" said Tammy, again. "It's getting bigger!"

He was pretty excited, and so was I.

I was peering down. The thing seemed to be rising out of the depths. It was taking shape. As I realised what the shape was, a queer, cold funk took me.

"See," said Tammy. "It's just like the shadow of a ship!"

And it was. The shadow of a ship rising out of the unexplored immensity beneath our keel. Plummer, who had not yet gone forrard, caught Tammy's last remark, and glanced over.

"What's 'e mean?" he asked.

"That!" replied Tammy, and pointed.

I jabbed my elbow into his ribs; but it was too late. Plummer had seen. Curiously enough, though, he seemed to think nothing of it.

"That ain't nothin', 'cept ther shadder er ther ship," he said.

Tammy, after my hint, let it go at that. But when Plummer had gone forrard with the others, I told him not to go telling everything round the decks, like that.

"We've got to be thundering careful!" I remarked. "You know what the Old

Man said, last watch!"

"Yes," said Tammy. "I wasn't thinking; I'll be careful next time."

A little way from me the Second Mate was still staring down into the water. I turned, and spoke to him.

"What do you make it out to be, Sir?" I asked.

"God knows!" he said, with a quick glance round to see whether any of the men were about.

He got down from the rail, and turned to go up on to the poop. At the top of the ladder, he leant over the break.

"You may as well ship that gangway, you two," he told us. "And mind, Jessop, keep your mouth shut about this."

"i, i, Sir," I answered.

"And you too, youngster!" he added and went aft along the poop.

Tammy and I were busy with the gangway when the Second came back. He had brought the Skipper.

"Right under the gangway, Sir" I heard the Second say, and he pointed down into the water.

For a little while, the Old Man stared. Then I heard him speak.

"I don't see anything," he said.

At that, the Second Mate bent more forward and peered down. So did I; but the thing, whatever it was, had gone completely.

"It's gone, Sir," said the Second. "It was there right enough when I came for you."

About a minute later, having finished shipping the gangway, I was going forrard, when the Second's voice called me back

"Tell the Captain what it was you saw just now," he said, in a low voice.

"I can't say exactly, Sir," I replied. "But it seemed to me like the shadow of a ship, rising up through the water."

"There, Sir," remarked the Second Mate to the Old Man. "Just what I told you."

The Skipper stared at me.

"You're quite sure?" he asked.

"Yes, Sir," I answered. "Tammy saw it, too."

I waited a minute. Then they turned to go aft. The Second was saying something.

"Can I go, Sir?" I asked.

"Yes, that will do, Jessop," he said, over his shoulder. But the Old Man came back to the break, and spoke to me.

"Remember, not a word of this forrard!" he said.

"No Sir," I replied, and he went back to the Second Mate; while I walked forrard to the fo'cas'le to get something to eat.

"Your whack's in the kettle, Jessop," said Tom, as I stepped in over the washboard. "An' I got your lime-juice in a pannikin."

"Thanks," I said, and sat down.

As I stowed away my grub, I took no notice of the chatter of the others. I was too stuffed with my own thoughts. That shadow of a vessel rising, you know, out of the profound deeps, had impressed me tremendously. It had not been imagination. Three of us had seen it—really four; for Plummer distinctly saw it; though he failed to recognise it as anything extraordinary.

As you can understand, I thought a lot about this shadow of a vessel. But, I am sure, for a time, my ideas must just have gone in an everlasting, blind circle. And then I got another thought; for I got thinking of the figures I had seen aloft in the early morning; and I began to imagine fresh things. You see, that first thing that had come up over the side, had come out of the sea. And it had gone back. And now there was this shadow vessel-thing—ghost-ship I called it. It was a damned good name, too. And the dark, noiseless men ... I thought a lot on these lines. Unconsciously, I put a question to myself, aloud:

"Were they the crew?"

"Eh?" said Jaskett, who was on the next chest.

I took hold of myself, as it were, and glanced at him, in an apparently careless manner.

"Did I speak?" I asked.

"Yes, mate," he replied, eyeing me, curiously. "Yer said sumthin' about a crew."

"I must have been dreaming," I said; and rose up to put away my plate.

THE GHOST SHIPS

At four o'clock, when again we went on deck, the Second Mate told me to go on with a paunch mat I was making; while Tammy, he sent to get out his sinnet. I had the mat slug on the fore side of the mainmast, between it and the after end of the house; and, in a few minutes, Tammy brought his sinnet and yarns to the mast, and made fast to one of the pins.

"What do you think it was, Jessop?" he asked, abruptly, after a short silence.

I looked at him.

"What do you think?" I replied.

"I don't know what to think," he said. "But I've a feeling that it's something to do with all the rest," and he indicated aloft, with his head.

"I've been thinking, too," I remarked.

"That it is?" he inquired.

"Yes," I answered, and told him how the idea had come to me at my dinner, that the strange men-shadows which came aboard, might come from that indistinct vessel we had seen down in the sea.

"Good Lord!" he exclaimed, as he got my meaning. And then for a little, he stood and thought.

"That's where they live, you mean?" he said, at last, and paused again.

"Well," I replied. "It can't be the sort of existence we should call life."

He nodded, doubtfully.

"No," he said, and was silent again.

Presently, he put out an idea that had come to him.

"You think, then, that that—vessel has been with us for some time, if we'd only known?" he asked.

"All along," I replied. "I mean ever since these things started."

"Supposing there are others," he said, suddenly.

I looked at him.

"If there are," I said. "You can pray to God that they won't stumble across us. It strikes me that whether they're ghosts, or not ghosts, they're blood-gutted pirates.

"It seems horrible," he said solemnly, "to be talking seriously like this, about—you know, about such things."

"I've tried to stop thinking that way," I told him. "I've felt I should go cracked, if I didn't. There's damned queer things happen at sea, I know; but this isn't one of them."

"It seems so strange and unreal, one moment, doesn't it?" he said. "And the next, you know it's really true, and you can't understand why you didn't always know. And yet they'd never believe, if you told them ashore about it."

"They'd believe, if they'd been in this packet in the middle watch this morning," I said.

"Besides," I went on. "They don't understand. We didn't ... I shall always feel different now, when I read that some packet hasn't been heard of."

Tammy stared at me.

"I've heard some of the old shellbacks talking about things," he said. "But I never took them really seriously."

"Well," I said. "I guess we'll have to take this seriously. I wish to God we were home!"

"My God! so do I," he said.

For a good while after that, we both worked on in silence; but, presently, he went off on another tack.

"Do you think we'll really shorten her down every night before it gets dark?" he asked.

"Certainly," I replied. "They'll never get the men to go aloft at night, after what's happened."

"But, but—supposing they ordered us aloft—" he began.

"Would you go?" I interrupted.

"No!" he said, emphatically. "I'd jolly well be put in irons first!"

"That settles it, then," I replied. "You wouldn't go, nor would any one else."

At this moment the Second Mate came along.

"Shove that mat and that sinnet away, you two," he said. "Then get your brooms and clear up."

"i, i, Sir," we said, and he went on forrard.

"Jump on the house, Tammy," I said. "And let go the other end of this rope, will you?"

"Right" he said, and did as I had asked him. When he came back, I got him to give me a hand to roll up the mat, which was a very large one.

"I'll finish stopping it," I said. "You go and put your sinnet away."

"Wait a minute," he replied, and gathered up a double handful of shakins from the deck, under where I had been working. Then he ran to the side.

"Here!" I said. "Don't go dumping those. They'll only float, and the Second Mate or the Skipper will be sure to spot them."

"Come here, Jessop!" he interrupted, in a low voice, and taking no notice of what I had been saying.

I got up off the hatch, where I was kneeling. He was staring over the side.

"What's up?" I asked.

"For God's sake, hurry!" he said, and I ran, and jumped on to the spar, alongside of him.

"Look!" he said, and pointed with a handful of shakins, right down, directly beneath us.

Some of the shakins dropped from his hand, and blurred the water, momentarily, so that I could not see. Then, as the ripples cleared away, I saw what he meant.

"Two of them!" he said, in a voice that was scarcely above a whisper. "And there's another out there," and he pointed again with the handful of shakins.

"There's another a little further aft," I muttered.

"Where?—where?" he asked.

"There," I said, and pointed.

"That's four," he whispered. "Four of them!"

I said nothing; but continued to stare. They appeared to me to be a great way down in the sea, and quite motionless. Yet, though their outlines were somewhat blurred and indistinct, there was no mistaking that they were very like exact, though shadowy, representations of vessels. For some minutes we watched them, without speaking. At last Tammy spoke.

"They're real, right enough," he said, in a low voice.

"I don't know," I answered.

"I mean we weren't mistaken this morning," he said.

"No," I replied. "I never thought we were."

Away forrard, I heard the Second Mate, returning aft. He came nearer, and saw us.

"What's up now, you two?" he called, sharply. "This isn't clearing up!"

I put out my hand to warn him not to shout, and draw the attention of the rest of the men.

He took several steps towards me.

"What is it? what is it?" he said, with a certain irritability; but in a lower voice.

"You'd better take a look over the side, Sir," I replied.

My tone must have given him an inkling that we had discovered something fresh; for, at my words, he made one spring, and stood on the spar, alongside of me.

"Look, Sir," said Tammy. "There's four of them."

The Second Mate glanced down, saw something and bent sharply forward.

"My God!" I heard him mutter, under his breath.

After that, for some half-minute, he stared, without a word.

"There are two more out there, Sir," I told him, and indicated the place with my finger.

It was a little time before he managed to locate these and when he did, he gave them only a short glance. Then he got down off the spar, and spoke to us.

"Come down off there," he said, quickly. "Get your brooms and clear up. Don't say a word!—It may be nothing."

He appeared to add that last bit, as an afterthought, and we both knew it meant nothing. Then he turned and went swiftly aft.

"I expect he's gone to tell the Old Man," Tammy remarked, as we went forrard, carrying the mat and his sinnet.

"H'm," I said, scarcely noticing what he was saying; for I was full of the thought of those four shadowy craft, waiting quietly down there.

We got our brooms, and went aft. On the way, the Second Mate and the Skipper passed us. They went forrard too by the fore brace, and got up on the spar. I saw the Second point up at the brace and he appeared to be saying something about the gear. I guessed that this was done purposely, to act as a blind, should any of the other men be looking. Then the Old Man glanced down over the side, in a casual sort of manner; so did the Second Mate. A minute or two later, they came aft, and went back, up on to the poop. I caught a glimpse of the Skipper's face as he passed me, on his return. He struck me as looking worried—bewildered, perhaps, would be a better word.

Both Tammy and I were tremendously keen to have another look; but when at last we got a chance, the sky reflected so much on the water, we could see nothing below.

We had just finished sweeping up when four bells went, and we cleared below for tea. Some of the men got chatting while they were grubbing.

"I 'ave 'eard," remarked Quoin, "as we're goin' ter shorten 'er down afore dark."

"Eh?" said old Jaskett, over his pannikin of tea.

Quoin repeated his remark.

"'oo says so?" inquired Plummer.

"I 'eard it from ther Doc," answered Quoin, "'e got it from ther Stooard."

"'ow would 'ee know?" asked Plummer.

"I dunno," said Quoin. "I 'spect 'e's 'eard 'em talkin' 'bout it arft."

Plummer turned to me.

"'ave you 'eard anythin', Jessop?" he inquired.

"What, about shortening down?" I replied.

"Yes," he said. "Weren't ther Old Man talkin' ter yer, up on ther poop this mornin'?"

"Yes," I answered. "He said something to the Second Mate about shortening down; but it wasn't to me."

"They are!" said Quoin, "'aven't I just said so?"

At that instant, one of the chaps in the other watch, poked his head in through the starboard doorway.

"All hands shorten sail!" he sung out; at the same moment the Mate's whistle came sharp along the decks.

Plummer stood up, and reached for his cap.

"Well," he said. "It's evydent they ain't goin' ter lose no more of us!"

Then we went out on deck.

It was a dead calm; but all the same, we furled the three royals, and then the three t'gallants. After that, we hauled up the main and foresail, and stowed them. The crossjack, of course, had been furled some time, with the wind being plumb aft.

It was while we were up at the foresail, that the sun went over the edge of the horizon. We had finished stowing the sail, out upon the yard, and I was waiting for the others to clear in, and let me get off the foot-rope. Thus it happened that having nothing to do for nearly a minute, I stood watching the sun set, and so saw something that otherwise I should, most probably, have missed. The sun had dipped nearly half-way below the horizon, and was showing like a great, red dome of dull fire. Abruptly, far away on the starboard bow, a faint mist drove up out of the sea. It spread across the face of the sun, so that its light shone now as though it came through a dim haze of smoke. Quickly, this mist or haze grew thicker; but, at the same time, separating and taking strange shapes, so that the red of the sun struck through ruddily between them. Then, as I watched, the weird mistiness collected and shaped and rose into three towers. These became more definite, and there was something elongated beneath them. The shaping and forming continued, and almost suddenly I saw that the thing had taken on the shape of a great ship. Directly afterwards, I saw that it was moving. It had been broadside on to the sun. Now it was swinging. The bows came round with a stately movement, until the three masts bore in a line. It was heading directly towards us. It grew larger; but yet less distinct. Astern of it, I saw now that the sun had sunk to a mere line of light. Then, in the gathering dusk it seemed to me that the ship was sinking back into the ocean. The sun went beneath the sea, and the thing I had seen became merged, as it were, into the monotonous greyness of the coming night.

A voice came to me from the rigging. It was the Second Mate's. He had been up to give us a hand.

"Now then, Jessop," he was saying. "Come along! come along!"

I turned quickly, and realised that the fellows were nearly all off the yard.

"i, i, Sir," I muttered, and slid in along the foot-rope, and went down on deck. I felt fresh dazed and frightened.

A little later, eight bells went, and, after roll call, I cleared up, on to the poop, to relieve the wheel. For a while as I stood at the wheel my mind seemed blank, and incapable of receiving impressions. This sensation went, after a time, and I realised that there was a great stillness over the sea. There was absolutely no wind, and even the everlasting creak, creak of the gear seemed to ease off at times.

At the wheel there was nothing whatever to do. I might just as well have been forrard, smoking in the fo'cas'le. Down on the main-deck, I could see the loom of the lanterns that had been lashed up to the sherpoles in the fore and main rigging. Yet they showed less than they might, owing to the fact that they had been shaded on their after sides, so as not to blind the officer of the watch more than need be.

The night had come down strangely dark, and yet of the dark and the stillness and the lanterns, I was only conscious in occasional flashes of comprehension. For, now that my mind was working, I was thinking chiefly of that queer, vast phantom of mist, I had seen rise from the sea, and take shape.

I kept staring into the night, towards the West, and then all round me; for, naturally, the memory predominated that she had been coming towards us when the darkness came, and it was a pretty disquieting sort of thing to think about. I had such a horrible feeling that something beastly was going to happen any minute.

Yet, two bells came and went, and still all was quiet—strangely quiet, it seemed to me. And, of course, besides the queer, misty vessel I had seen in the West I was all the time remembering the four shadowy craft lying down in the sea, under our port side. Every time I remembered them, I felt thankful for the lanterns round the maindeck, and I wondered why none had been put in the mizzen rigging. I wished to goodness that they had, and made up my mind I would speak to the Second Mate about it, next time he came aft. At the time, he was leaning over the rail across the break of the poop. He was not smoking, as I could tell; for had he been, I should have seen the glow of his pipe, now and then. It was plain to me that he was uneasy. Three times already he had been down on to the maindeck, prowling about. I guessed that he had been to look down into the sea, for any signs of those four grim craft. I wondered whether they would be visible at night.

Suddenly, the time-keeper struck three bells, and the deeper notes of the bell forrard, answered them. I gave a start. It seemed to me that they had been struck close to my elbow. There was something unaccountably strange in the air that night. Then, even as the Second Mate answered the look-out's "All's well," there came the sharp whir and rattle of running gear, on the port side of the mainmast. Simultaneously, there was the shrieking of a parrel, up the main; and I knew that someone, or something, had let go the main-topsail haul-yards. From aloft there came the sound of something parting; then the crash of the yard as it ceased falling.

The Second Mate shouted out something unintelligible, and jumped for the ladder. From the maindeck there came the sound of running feet, and the voices of the watch, shouting. Then I caught the Skipper's voice; he must have run out on deck, through the Saloon doorway.

"Get some more lamps! Get some more lamps!" he was singing out. Then he swore.

He sung out something further. I caught the last two words.

"...carried away," they sounded like.

"No, Sir," shouted the Second Mate. "I don't think so."

A minute of some confusion followed; and then came the click of pawls. I could tell that they had taken the haulyards to the after capstan. Odd words floated up to me.

"...all this water?" I heard in the Old Man's voice. He appeared to be asking a question.

"Can't say, Sir," came the Second Mate's.

There was a period of time, filled only by the clicking of the pawls and the sounds of the creaking parrel and the running gear. Then the Second Mate's voice came again.

"Seems all right, Sir," I heard him say.

I never heard the Old Man's reply; for in the same moment, there came to me a chill of cold breath at my back. I turned sharply, and saw something peering over the taffrail. It had eyes that reflected the binnacle light, weirdly, with a frightful, tigerish gleam; but beyond that, I could see nothing with any distinctness. For the moment, I just stared. I seemed frozen. It was so close. Then movement came to me, and I jumped to the binnacle and snatched out the lamp. I twitched round, and shone the light towards it. The thing, whatever it was, had come more forward over the rail; but now, before the light, it recoiled with a queer, horrible litheness. It slid back, and down, and so out of sight. I have only a confused notion of a wet glistening Something, and two vile eyes. Then I was running, crazy, towards the break of the poop. I sprang down the ladder, and missed my footing, and landed on my stern, at the bottom. In my left hand I held the still burning binnacle lamp. The men were putting away the capstan-bars; but at my abrupt appearance, and the yell I gave out at falling, one or two of them fairly ran backwards a short distance, in sheer funk, before they realised what it was.

From somewhere further forrard, the Old Man and the Second Mate came running aft.

"What the devil's up now?" sung out the Second, stopping and bending to stare at me. "What's to do, that you're away from the wheel?"

I stood up and tried to answer him; but I was so shaken that I could only stammer.

"I—I—there—" I stuttered.

"Damnation!" shouted the Second Mate, angrily. "Get back to the wheel!"

I hesitated, and tried to explain.

"Do you damned well hear me?" he sung out.

"Yes, Sir; but—" I began.

"Get up on to the poop, Jessop!" he said.

I went. I meant to explain, when he came up. At the top of the ladder, I stopped. I was not going back alone to that wheel. Down below, I heard the Old Man speaking.

"What on earth is it now, Mr. Tulipson?" he was saying.

The Second Mate made no immediate reply; but turned to the men, who were evidently crowding near.

"That will do, men!" he said, somewhat sharply.

I heard the watch start to go forrard. There came a mutter of talk from them. Then the Second Mate answered the Old Man. He could not have known that I was near enough to overhear him.

"It's Jessop, Sir. He must have seen something; but we mustn't frighten the crowd more than need be."

"No," said the Skipper's voice.

They turned and came up the ladder, and I ran back a few steps, as far as the skylight. I heard the Old Man speak as they came up.

"How is it there are no lamps, Mr. Tulipson?" he said, in a surprised tone.

"I thought there would be no need up here, Sir," the Second Mate replied. Then he added something about saving oil.

"Better have them, I think," I heard the Skipper say.

"Very good, Sir," answered the Second, and sung out to the time-keeper to bring up a couple of lamps.

Then the two of them walked aft, to where I stood by the skylight.

"What are you doing, away from the wheel?" asked the Old Man, in a stern voice.

I had collected my wits somewhat by now.

"I won't go, Sir, till there's a light," I said.

The Skipper stamped his foot, angrily; but the Second Mate stepped forward.

"Come! Come, Jessop!" he exclaimed. "This won't do, you know! You'd better get back to the wheel without further bother."

"Wait a minute," said the Skipper, at this juncture. "What objection have you to going back to the wheel?" he asked.

"I saw something," I said. "It was climbing over the taffrail, Sir—"

"Ah!" he said, interrupting me with a quick gesture. Then, abruptly: "Sit down! sit down; you're all in a shake, man."

I flopped down on to the skylight seat. I was, as he had said, all in a shake, and the binnacle lamp was wobbling in my hand, so that the light from it went dancing here and there across the deck.

"Now," he went on. "Just tell us what you saw."

I told them, at length, and while I was doing so, the time-keeper brought up the lights and lashed one up on the sheerpole in each rigging.

"Shove one under the spanker boom," the Old Man sung out, as the boy finished lashing up the other two. "Be smart now."

"i, i, Sir," said the 'prentice, and hurried off.

"Now then," remarked the Skipper when this had been done "You needn't be afraid to go back to the wheel. There's a light over the stern, and the Second Mate or myself will be up here all the time."

I stood up.

"Thank you, Sir," I said, and went aft. I replaced my lamp in the binnacle, and took hold of the wheel; yet, time and again, I glanced behind and I was very thankful when, a few minutes later, four bells went, and I was relieved.

Though the rest of the chaps were forrard in the fo'cas'le, I did not go there. I shirked being questioned about my sudden appearance at the foot of the poop ladder; and so I lit my pipe and wandered about the maindeck. I did not feel particularly nervous, as there were now two lanterns in each rigging, and a couple standing upon each of the spare top-masts under the bulwarks.

Yet, a little after five bells, it seemed to me that I saw a shadowy face peer over the rail, a little abaft the fore lanyards. I snatched up one of the lanterns from off the spar, and flashed the light towards it, whereupon there was nothing. Only, on my mind, more than my sight, I fancy, a queer knowledge remained of wet, peery eyes. Afterwards, when I thought about them, I felt extra beastly. I knew then how brutal they had been ... Inscrutable, you know. Once more in that same watch I had a somewhat similar experience, only in this instance it had vanished even before I had time to reach a light. And then came eight bells, and our watch below.

THE GREAT GHOST SHIP

When we were called again, at a quarter to four, the man who roused us out, had some queer information.

"Toppin's gone—clean vanished!" he told us, as we began to turn out. "I never was in such a damned, hair-raisin' hooker as this here. It ain't safe to go about the bloomin' decks."

"'oo's gone?" asked Plummer, sitting up suddenly and throwing his legs over his bunk-board.

"Toppin, one of the 'prentices," replied the man. "We've been huntin' all over the bloomin' show. We're still at it—but we'll never find him," he ended, with a sort of gloomy assurance.

"Oh, I dunno," said Quoin. "P'raps 'e's snoozin' somewheres 'bout."

"Not him," replied the man. "I tell you we've turned everythin' upside down. He's not aboard the bloomin' ship.

"Where was he when they last saw him?" I asked.

"Someone must know something, you know!"

"Keepin' time up on the poop," he replied. "The Old Man's nearly shook the life out of the Mate and the chap at the wheel. And they say they don't know nothin'."

"How do you mean?" I inquired. "How do you mean, nothing?"

"Well," he answered. "The youngster was there one minute, and then the next thing they knew, he'd gone. They've both sworn black an' blue that there wasn't a whisper. He's just disappeared off of the face of the bloomin' earth."

I got down on to my chest, and reached for my boots.

Before I could speak again, the man was saying something fresh.

"See here, mates," he went on. "If things is goin' on like this, I'd like to know where you an' me'll be befor' long!"

"We'll be in 'ell," said Plummer.

"I dunno as I like to think 'bout it," said Quoin.

"We'll have to think about it!" replied the man. "We've got to think a bloomin' lot about it. I've talked to our side, an' they're game."

"Game for what?" I asked.

"To go an' talk straight to the bloomin' Capting," he said, wagging his finger at me. "It's make tracks for the nearest bloomin' port, an' don't you make no bloomin' mistake."

I opened my mouth to tell him that the probability was we should not be able to make it, even if he could get the Old Man to see the matter from his point of view. Then I remembered that the chap had no idea of the things I had seen, and thought out; so, instead, I said:

"Supposing he won't?"

"Then we'll have to bloomin' well make him," he replied.

"And when you got there," I said. "What then? You'd be jolly well locked up for mutiny."

"I'd sooner be locked up," he said. "It don't kill you!"

There was a murmur of agreement from the others, and then a moment of silence, in which, I know, the men were thinking.

Jaskett's voice broke into it.

"I never thought at first as she was 'aunted—" he commenced; but Plummer cut in across his speech.

"We mustn't 'urt any one, yer know," he said. "That'd mean 'angin', an' they ain't been er bad crowd.

"No," assented everyone, including the chap who had come to call us.

"All the same," he added. "It's got to be up hellum, an' shove her into the nearest bloomin' port."

"Yes," said everyone, and then eight bells went, and we cleared out on deck.

Presently, after roll-call—in which there had come a queer, awkward little pause at Toppin's name—Tammy came over to me. The rest of the men had gone forrard, and I guessed they were talking over mad plans for forcing the Skipper's hand, and making him put into port—poor beggars!

I was leaning over the port rail, by the fore brace-lock, staring down into the sea, when Tammy came to me. For perhaps a minute he said nothing. When at last he spoke, it was to say that the shadow vessels had not been there since daylight.

"What?" I said, in some surprise. "How do you know?"

"I woke up when they were searching for Toppin," he replied. "I've not been asleep since. I came here, right away." He began to say something further; but stopped short.

"Yes," I said encouragingly.

"I didn't know—" he began, and broke off. He caught my arm. "Oh, Jessop!" he exclaimed. "What's going to be the end of it all? Surely something can be done?"

I said nothing. I had a desperate feeling that there was very little we could do to help ourselves.

"Can't we do something?" he asked, and shook my arm. "Anything's better than this! We're being murdered!"

Still, I said nothing; but stared moodily down into the water. I could plan nothing; though I would get mad, feverish fits of thinking.

"Do you hear?" he said. He was almost crying.

"Yes, Tammy," I replied. "But I don't know! I don't know!"

"You don't know!" he exclaimed. "You don't know! Do you mean we're just to give in, and be murdered, one after another?"

"We've done all we can," I replied. "I don't know what else we can do, unless we go below and lock ourselves in, every night."

"That would be better than this," he said. "There'll be no one to go below, or anything else, soon!"

"But what if it came on to blow?" I asked. "We'd be having the sticks blown out of her."

"What if it came on to blow now?" he returned. "No one would go aloft, if it were dark, you said, yourself! Besides, we could shorten her right down, first. I tell you, in a few days there won't be a chap alive aboard this packet unless they jolly well do something!"

"Don't shout," I warned him. "You'll have the Old Man hearing you." But the young beggar was wound up, and would take no notice.

"I will shout," he replied. "I want the Old Man to hear. I've a good mind to go up and tell him."

He started on a fresh tack.

"Why don't the men do something?" he began. "They ought to damn well make the Old Man put us into port! They ought—"

"For goodness sake, shut up, you little fool!" I said. "What's the good of talking a lot of damned rot like that? You'll be getting yourself into trouble."

"I don't care," he replied. "I'm not going to be murdered!"

"Look here," I said. "I told you before, that we shouldn't be able to see the land, even if we made it."

"You've no proof," he answered. "It's only your idea."

"Well," I replied. "Proof, or no proof, the Skipper would only pile her up, if he tried to make the land, with things as they are now."

"Let him pile her up," he answered. "Let him jolly well pile her up! That would be better than staying out here to be pulled overboard, or chucked down from aloft!"

"Look here, Tammy—" I began; but just then the Second Mate sung out for him, and he had to go. When he came back, I had started to walk to and from, across the fore side of the mainmast. He joined me, and after a minute, he started his wild talk again.

"Look here, Tammy," I said, once more. "It's no use your talking like you've been doing. Things are as they are, and it's no one's fault, and nobody can help it. If you want to talk sensibly, I'll listen; if not, then go and gas to someone else."

With that, I returned to the port side, and got up on the spar, again, intending to sit on the pinrail and have a bit of a talk with him. Before sitting down I glanced over, into the sea. The action had been almost mechanical; yet, after a few instants, I was in a state of the most intense excitement, and without withdrawing my gaze, I reached out and caught Tammy's arm to attract his attention.

"My God!" I muttered. "Look!"

"What is it?" he asked, and bent over the rail, beside me. And this is what we saw: a little distance below the surface there lay a pale-coloured, slightly-domed disc. It seemed only a few feet down. Below it, we saw quite clearly, after a few moment's staring, the shadow of a royal-yard, and, deeper, the gear and standing-rigging of a great mast. Far down among the shadows I thought, presently, that I could make out the immense, indefinite stretch of vast decks.

"My God!" whispered Tammy, and shut up. But presently, he gave out a short exclamation, as though an idea had come to him; and got down off the spar, and ran forrard on to the fo'cas'le head. He came running back, after a short look into the sea, to tell me that there was the truck of another great mast coming up there, a bit off the bow, to within a few feet of the surface of the sea.

In the meantime, you know, I had been staring like mad down through the water at the huge, shadowy mast just below me. I had traced out bit by bit, until now I could clearly see the jackstay, running along the top of the royal mast; and, you know, the royal itself was set.

But, you know, what was getting at me more than anything, was a feeling that there was movement down in the water there, among the rigging. I thought I could actually see, at times, things moving and glinting faintly and rapidly to and fro in the gear. And once, I was practically certain that something was on the royal-yard, moving in to the mast; as though, you know, it might have come up the leech of the sail. And this way, I got a beastly feeling that there were things swarming down there.

Unconsciously, I must have leant further and further out over the side, staring; and suddenly—good Lord! how I yelled—I overbalanced. I made a sweeping grab, and caught the fore brace, and with that, I was back in a moment upon the spar. In the same second, almost, it seemed to me that the surface of the water above the submerged truck was broken, and I am sure now, I saw something a moment in the air against the ship's side —a sort of shadow in the air; though I did not realise it at the time. Anyway, the next instant, Tammy gave out an awful scream, and was head downwards over the rail, in a second. I had an idea then that he was jumping overboard. I collared him by the waist of his britchers, and one knee, and then I had him down on the deck, and sat plump on him; for he was struggling and shouting all the time, and I was so breathless and shaken and gone to mush, I could not have trusted my hands to hold him. You see, I never thought then it was anything but some influence at work on him; and that he was trying to get loose to go over the side. But I know now that I saw the shadow-man that had him. Only, at the time, I was so mixed up, and with the one idea in my head, I was not really able to notice anything, properly. But, afterwards, I comprehended a bit (you can understand, can't you?) what I had seen at the time without taking in.

And even now looking back, I know that the shadow was only like a faint-seen greyness in the daylight, against the whiteness of the decks, clinging against Tammy.

And there was I, all breathless and sweating, and quivery with my own tumble, sitting on the little screeching beggar, and he fighting like a mad thing; so that I thought I should never hold him.

And then I heard the Second Mate shouting and there came running feet along the deck. Then many hands were pulling and hauling, to get me off him.

"Bl—y cowyard!" sung out someone.

"Hold him! Hold him!" I shouted. "He'll be overboard!"

At that, they seemed to understand that I was not ill-treating the youngster; for they stopped manhandling me, and allowed me to rise; while two of them took hold of Tammy, and kept him safe.

"What's the matter with him?" the Second Mate was singing out. "What's happened?"

"He's gone off his head, I think," I said.

"What?" asked the Second Mate. But before I could answer him, Tammy ceased suddenly to struggle, and flopped down upon the deck.

"'e's fainted," said Plummer, with some sympathy. He looked at me, with a puzzled, suspicious air. "What's 'appened? What's 'e been doin'?"

"Take him aft into the berth!" ordered the Second Mate, a bit abruptly. It struck me that he wished to prevent questions. He must have tumbled to the fact that we had seen something, about which it would be better not to tell the crowd.

Plummer stooped to lift the boy.

"No," said the Second Mate. "Not you, Plummer. Jessop, you take him." He turned to the rest of the men. "That will do," he told them and they went forrard, muttering a little.

I lifted the boy, and carried him aft.

"No need to take him into the berth," said the Second Mate. "Put him down on the after hatch. I've sent the other lad for some brandy."

Then the brandy came, we dosed Tammy and soon brought him round. He sat up, with a somewhat dazed air. Otherwise, he seemed quiet and sane enough.

"What's up?" he asked. He caught sight of the Second Mate. "Have I been ill, Sir?" he exclaimed.

"You're right enough now, youngster," said the Second Mate. "You've been a bit off. You'd better go and lie down for a bit."

"I'm all right now, Sir," replied Tammy. "I don't think—"

"You do as you're told!" interrupted the Second. "Don't always have to be told twice! If I want you, I'll send for you."

Tammy stood up, and made his way, in rather an unsteady fashion, into the berth. I fancy he was glad enough to lie down.

"Now then, Jessop," exclaimed the Second Mate, turning to me. "What's been the cause of all this? Out with it now, smart!"

I commenced to tell him; but, almost directly, he put up his hand.

"Hold on a minute," he said. "There's the breeze!"

He jumped up the port ladder, and sung out to the chap at the wheel. Then down again.

"Starboard fore brace," he sung out. He turned to me. "You'll have to finish telling me afterwards," he said.

"i, i, Sir," I replied, and went to join the other chaps at the braces.

As soon as we were braced sharp up on the port tack, he sent some of the watch up to loose the sails. Then he sung out for me.

"Go on with your yarn now, Jessop," he said.

I told him about the great shadow vessel, and I said something about Tammy—I mean about my not being sure now whether he had tried to jump overboard. Because, you see, I began to realise that I had seen the shadow; and I remembered the stirring of the water above the submerged truck. But the Second did not wait, of course, for any theories, but was away, like a shot, to see for himself. He ran to the side, and looked down. I followed, and stood beside him; yet, now that the surface of the water was blurred by the wind, we could see nothing.

"It's no good," he remarked, after a minute. "You'd better get away from the rail before any of the others see you. Just be taking those halyards aft to the capstan."

From then, until eight bells, we were hard at work getting the sail upon her, and when at last eight bells went, I made haste to swallow my breakfast, and get a sleep.

At midday, when we went on deck for the afternoon watch, I ran to the side; but there was no sign of the great shadow ship. All that watch, the Second Mate kept me working at my paunch mat, and Tammy he put on to his sinnet, telling me to keep an eye on the youngster. But the boy was right enough; as I scarcely doubted now, you know; though—a most unusual thing—he hardly opened his lips the whole afternoon. Then at four o'clock, we went below for tea.

At four bells, when we came on deck again, I found that the light breeze, which had kept us going during the day, had dropped, and we were only just moving. The sun was low down, and the sky clear. Once or twice, as I glanced across to the horizon, it seemed to me that I caught again that odd quiver in the air that had preceded the coming of the mist; and, indeed on two separate occasions, I saw a thin whisp of haze drive up, apparently out of the sea. This was at some little distance on our port beam; otherwise, all was quiet and peaceful; and though I stared into the water, I could make out no vestige of that great shadow ship, down in the sea.

It was some little time after six bells that the order came for all hands to shorten sail for the night. We took in the royals and t'gallants, and then the three courses. It was shortly after this, that a rumour went round the ship that there was to be no look-out that night after eight o'clock. This naturally created a good deal of talk among the men; especially as the yarn went that the fo'cas'le doors were to be shut and fastened as soon as it was dark, and that no one was to be allowed on deck.

"'oo's goin' ter take ther wheel?" I heard Plummer ask.

"I s'pose they'll 'ave us take 'em as usual," replied one of the men. "One of ther officers is bound ter be on ther poop; so we'll 'ave company."

Apart from these remarks, there was a general opinion that—if it were true—it was a sensible act on the part of the Skipper. As one of the men said:

"It ain't likely that there'll be any of us missin' in ther mornin', if we stays in our bunks all ther blessed night."

And soon after this, eight bells went.

The Ghost Pirates

At the moment when eight bells actually went, I was in the fo'cas'le, talking to four of the other watch. Suddenly, away aft, I heard shouting, and then on the deck overhead, came the loud thudding of someone pomping with a capstan-bar. Straightway, I turned and made a run for the port doorway, along with the four other men. We rushed out through the doorway on to the deck. It was getting dusk; but that did not hide from me a terrible and extraordinary sight. All along the port rail there was a queer, undulating greyness, that moved downwards inboard, and spread over the decks. As I looked, I found that I saw more clearly, in a most extraordinary way. And, suddenly, all the moving greyness resolved into hundreds of strange men. In the half-light, they looked unreal and impossible, as though there had come upon us the inhabitants of some fantastic dream-world. My God! I thought I was mad. They swarmed in upon us in a great wave of murderous, living shadows. From some of the men who must have been going aft for roll-call, there rose into the evening air a loud, awful shouting.

"Aloft!" yelled someone; but, as I looked aloft, I saw that the horrible things were swarming there in scores and scores.

"Jesus Christ—!" shrieked a man's voice, cut short, and my glance dropped from aloft, to find two of the men who had come out from the fo'cas'le with me, rolling upon the deck. They were two indistinguishable masses that writhed here and there across the planks. The brutes fairly covered them. From them, came muffled little shrieks and gasps; and there I stood, and with me were the other two men. A man darted past us into the fo'cas'le, with two grey men on his back, and I heard them kill him. The two men by me, ran suddenly across the fore hatch, and up the starboard ladder on to the fo'cas'le head. Yet, almost in the same instant, I saw several of the grey men disappear up the other ladder. From the fo'cas'le head above, I heard the two men commence to shout, and this died away into a loud scuffling. At that, I turned to see whether I could get away. I stared round, hopelessly; and then with two jumps, I was on the pigsty, and from there upon the top of the deckhouse. I threw myself flat, and waited, breathlessly.

All at once, it seemed to me that it was darker than it had been the previous moment, and I raised my head, very cautiously. I saw that the ship was enveloped in great billows of mist, and then, not six feet from me, I made out someone lying, face downwards. It was Tammy. I felt safer now that we were hidden by the mist, and I crawled to him. He gave a quick gasp of terror when I touched him; but when he saw who it was, he started to sob like a little kid.

"Hush!" I said. "For God's sake be quiet!" But I need not have troubled; for the shrieks of the men being killed, down on the decks all around us, drowned every other sound.

I knelt up, and glanced round and then aloft. Overhead, I could make out dimly the spars and sails, and now as I looked, I saw that the t'gallants and royals had been unloosed and were hanging in the buntlines. Almost in the same moment, the terrible crying of the poor beggars about the decks, ceased; and there succeeded an awful silence, in which I could distinctly hear Tammy sobbing. I reached out, and shook him.

"Be quiet! Be quiet!" I whispered, intensely. "THEY'LL hear us!"

At my touch and whisper, he struggled to become silent; and then, overhead, I saw the six yards being swiftly mast-headed. Scarcely were the sails set, when I heard the swish and flick of gaskets being cast adrift on the lower yards, and realised that ghostly things were at work there.

For a moment or so there was silence, and I made my way cautiously to the after end of the house, and peered over. Yet, because of the mist, I could see nothing. Then, abruptly, from behind me, came a single wail of sudden pain and terror from Tammy. It ended instantly in a sort of choke. I stood up in the mist and ran back to where I had left the kid; but he had gone. I stood dazed. I felt like shrieking out loud. Above me I heard the flaps of the course being tumbled off the yards. Down upon the decks, there were the noises of a multitude working in a weird, inhuman silence. Then came the squeal and rattle of blocks and braces aloft. They were squaring the yards.

I remained standing. I watched the yards squared, and then I saw the sails fill suddenly. An instant later, the deck of the house upon which I stood, became canted forrard. The slope increased, so that I could scarcely stand, and I grabbed at one of the wire-winches. I wondered, in a stunned sort of way, what was happening. Almost directly afterwards, from the deck on the port side of the house, there came a sudden, loud, human scream; and immediately, from different parts of the decks, there rose, afresh, some most horrible shouts of agony from odd men. This grew into an intense screaming that shook my heart up; and there came again a noise of desperate, brief fighting. Then a breath of cold wind seemed to play in the mist, and I could see down the slope of the deck. I looked below me,

towards the bows. The jibboom was plunged right into the water, and, as
I stared, the bows disappeared into the sea. The deck of the house became
a wall to me, and I was swinging from the winch, which was now above my
head. I watched the ocean lap over the edge of the fo'cas'le head, and rush
down on to the maindeck, roaring into the empty fo'cas'le. And still all
around me came crying of the lost sailor-men. I heard something strike the
corner of the house above me, with a dull thud, and then I saw Plummer
plunge down into the flood beneath. I remembered that he had been at the
wheel. The next instant, the water had leapt to my feet; there came a drear
chorus of bubbling screams, a roar of waters, and I was going swiftly down
into the darkness. I let go of the winch, and struck out madly, trying to
hold my breath. There was a loud singing in my ears. It grew louder. I
opened my mouth. I felt I was dying. And then, thank God! I was at the
surface, breathing. For the moment, I was blinded with the water, and my
agony of breathlessness. Then, growing easier, I brushed the water from my
eyes and so, not three hundred yards away, I made out a large ship, floating
almost motionless. At first, I could scarcely believe I saw aright. Then, as
I realised that indeed there was yet a chance of living, I started to swim
towards you.

You know the rest—

"And you think—?" said the Captain, interrogatively, and stopped short.

"No," replied Jessop. "I don't think. I _know. None of us think. It's a
gospel fact. People talk about queer things happening at sea; but this isn't
one of them. This is one of the real things. You've all seen queer things;
perhaps more than I have. It depends. But they don't go down in the log.
These kinds of things never do. This one won't; at least, not as it's really
happened."

He nodded his head, slowly, and went on, addressing the Captain more
particularly.

"I'll bet," he said, deliberately, "that you'll enter it in the log-book,
something like this:

"'May 18th. Lat.—S. Long.—W. 2 p.m. Light winds from the South and
East. Sighted a full-rigged ship on the starboard bow. Overhauled her in the
first dog-watch. Signalled her; but received no response. During the second
dog-watch she steadily refused to communicate. About eight bells, it was
observed that she seemed to be settling by the head, and a minute later she
foundered suddenly, bows foremost, with all her crew. Put out a boat and
picked up one of the men, an A.B. by the name of Jessop. He was quite
unable to give any explanation of the catastrophe.'

"And you two," he made a gesture at the First and Second Mates, "will probably sign your names to it, and so will I, and perhaps one of your A.B.s. Then when we get home they'll print a report of it in the newspapers, and people will talk about the unseaworthy ships. Maybe some of the experts will talk rot about rivets and defective plates and so forth."

He laughed, cynically. Then he went on.

"And you know, when you come to think of it, there's no one except our own selves will ever know how it happened—really. The shellbacks don't count. They're only 'beastly, drunken brutes of common sailors'—poor devils! No one would think of taking anything they said, as anything more than a damned cuffer. Besides, the beggars only tell these things when they're half-boozed. They wouldn't then (for fear of being laughed at), only they're not responsible—"

He broke off, and looked round at us.

The Skipper and the two Mates nodded their heads, in silent assent.

Appendix: The Silent Ship

I'm the Third Mate of the Sangier, the vessel that picked up Jessop, you know; and he's asked us to write a short note of what we saw from our side, and sign it. The Old Man's set me on the job, as he says I can put it better than he can.

Well, it was in the first dog-watch that we came up with her, the Mortzestus I mean; but it was in the second dog-watch that it happened. The Mate and I were on the poop watching her. You see, we'd signalled her, and she'd not taken any notice, and that seemed queer, as we couldn't have been more than three or four hundred yards off her port beam, and it was a fine evening; so that we could almost have had a tea-fight, if they'd seemed a pleasant crowd. As it was, we called them a set of sulky swine, and left it at that, though we still kept our hoist up.

All the same, you know, we watched her a lot; and I remember even then I thought it queer how quiet she was. We couldn't even hear her bell go and I spoke to the Mate about it, and he said he'd been noticing the same thing.

Then, about six bells they shortened her right down to top-sails; and I can tell you that made us stare more than ever, as anyone can imagine. And I remember we noticed then especially that we couldn't hear a single sound from her even when the haul yards were let go; and, you know, without the glass, I saw their Old Man singing out something; but we didn't get a sound of it and we should have been able to hear every word.

Then, just before eight bells, the thing Jessop's told us about happened. Both the Mate and the Old Man said they could see men going up her side a bit indistinct, you know, because it was getting dusk; but the Second Mate and I half thought we did and half thought we didn't; but there was something queer; we all knew that; and it looked like a sort of moving mist along her side. I know I felt pretty funny; but it wasn't the sort of thing, of course, to be too sure and serious about until you were sure.

After the Mate and the Captain had said they saw the men boarding her, we began to hear sounds from her; very queer at first and rather like a phonograph makes when it's getting up speed. Then the sounds came properly from her, and we heard them shouting and yelling; and, you know, I don't know even now just what I really thought. I was all so queer and mixed.

The next thing I remember there was a thick mist round the ship; and then all the noise was shut off, as if it were all the other side of a door. But we could still see her masts and spars and sails above the misty stuff; and both the Captain and the Mate said they could see men aloft; and I thought I could; but the Second Mate wasn't sure. All the same though, the sails were all loosed in about a minute, it seemed, and the yards mastheaded. We couldn't see the courses above the mist; but Jessop says they were loosed too and sheeted home along with the upper sails. Then we saw the yards squared and I saw the sails fill bang up with wind; and yet, you know, ours were slatting.

The next thing was the one that hit me more than anything. Her masts took a cant forrard, and then I saw her stem come up out of the mist that was round her. Then, all in an instant, we could hear sounds from the vessel again. And I tell you, the men didn't seem to be shouting, but screaming. Her stern went higher. It was most extraordinary to look at; and then she went plunk down, head foremost, right bang into the mist-stuff.

It's all right what Jessop says, and when we saw him swimming (I was the one who spotted him) we got out a boat quicker than a wind-jammer ever got out a boat before, I should think.

The Captain and the Mate and the Second and I are all going to sign this.

(Signed)

WILLIAM NAWSTON Master.

J.E.G. ADAMS First Mate.

ED. BROWN Second Mate.

JACK T. EVAN Third Mate.